This book should be returned to any branch of the Lancashire County Library on or before the date shown

FORTRESS EL ZEEB

An Arab rolled a deserter's head in the sand, waiting for his reward, in the desert fortress of El Zeeb . . . Every legionnaire became suspicious of his neighbour and hatred led to other severed heads rolling. First to follow was that of Captain Paon, the Commander. The murder seemed impossible: his room was locked from within; there was a thirty-foot drop from the window; and the tower, detached from the fortress, was under constant surveillance by a guard.

GORDON LANDSBOROUGH

———————◆———————

FORTRESS EL ZEEB

Complete and Unabridged

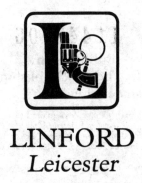

LINFORD
Leicester

First published in Great Britain

First Linford Edition
published 2010

British Library CIP Data

Landsborough, Gordon.
  Fortress El Zeeb.- -(Linford mystery library)
  1. Detective and mystery stories.
  2. Large type books.
  I. Title II. Series
  823.9'14–dc22

  ISBN 978–1–44480–220–7

11448706
Published by
F. A. Thorpe (Publishing)
Anstey, Leicestershire

Set by Words & Graphics Ltd.
Anstey, Leicestershire
Printed and bound in Great Britain by
T. J. International Ltd., Padstow, Cornwall

This book is printed on acid-free paper

1

Dust Devils

By four in the afternoon there were dust devils everywhere, whirling madly across the desert like dancing Dervishes, springing into brief life as the low-moaning wind freshened, then settling between gusts into the sand that was their origin.

It was a wind that had crossed a thousand hot miles of arid Sahara, so that when it came to the tiny hill on which stood the fortress of El Zeeb, it whipped the skin like the back blast from a blowlamp. In direct line with it, at his post over the stout wooden main gate, was Legionnaire Henri Putôt, The Paralysed One.

Perhaps the choice was fortunate, for The Paralysed One could stand with his right cheek to the blast and feel not a thing — there were compensations for having one's head cut open by an Arab sword, resulting in facial paralysis of the

1

right side. Not many, but some, as now.

Needle-pointed desert sand was whipping up from the earth-grey desert, so unlike the cleaner, even-grained yellowness beyond the low foothills where the Arab villages lay. But that, too, had no effect upon The Paralysed One, not while he showed his profile to the blast.

But there is a disadvantage to keeping watch in this manner. There is the important matter of focusing, which cannot successfully be accomplished with one eye, not in a desert that is shifting with heat haze, and spotted with rapid-moving, man-sized swirls of dust — the dust devils that grow out of the desert whenever a wind stirs.

So it was that the Arabs came to within three hundred yards of the fort before The Paralysed One caught the movement with his better eye. Immediately his rifle came up from the ground, and in one smooth, practised movement, the butt was hard against his right shoulder, sights were levelled and the first pressure taken on the trigger of the Lebel.

Simultaneously the good muscles of his

2

left cheek fought against the paralysed right cheek to get his mouth open in a shout of warning — it gaped lop-sided but his cry came ringing clearly, compellingly out, all the same. '*Caporal! Ici . . .*' And then his voice changed as he saw that this was no surprise attack; for on the desert trail outside there were three Arabs and a donkey, and one of the Arabs but a child at that.

The corporal of the guard came running out of the guardhouse, his shadow squat and very dark because of the intensity of light from the African summer sun.

'*Qu'y a-t-il?*' Other legionnaires were coming to the doors of the barrack rooms, that sharp, unexpected cry crackling through their dozing consciousness and jerking them rudely from the debatable comfort of siesta.

'What's the matter?' repeated the corporal and the way he said it promised ill for the good Henri if there were not sufficient reason for his quick alarm.

The Paralysed One was full-faced towards the wind now, watching. They heard him call . . . '*Trois Arabi et une ane!*'

'Three Arabs and a donkey?' roared the corporal. To be awakened from sleep for such a thing, indeed! 'O thou donkey, thou shalt learn the manners of discretion!' he shouted passionately, only he expressed it differently and at greater length and with a degree of coarseness not unusual among corporals of seven years' service in the Foreign Legion.

But The Paralysed One was unperturbed. He could see something else, and as he heard the corporal's threats he just shook his head.

The corporal came swearing along the battlement and peered through the embrasure; then he dropped quickly into the dust of the parade ground and ran across to the officers' quarters. No longer did he make threats to The Paralysed One, no longer did he complain about the abrupt termination of a siesta to which a guard commander is not entitled, anyway, and for which theoretically he deserves to be shot.

At that phenomenon, a whisper ran

through the barrack rooms and now all the legionnaires rose and came to the doors and windows and looked out, expectant and quietly waiting.

At his post The Paralysed One had dropped his rifle but his eyes were no less bleak and hostile, watching the Arabs approach. And they seemed to sense it, and were uneasy and came along slowly.

One led the donkey, with the small Arab child trotting beside him; the third sat back on the beast, and held a brown sack-like bundle before him. It was upon that bundle that the eyes of Legionnaire Henri Putôt were fixed.

Two hundred yards away, the Arabs stopped and for a while squatted together in the dust, as if afraid to come farther without assuring words from each other. And all the time they talked, and their uneasy eyes never left the fort with that sentry right before them with his rifle held so menacingly.

At last they made a move, and once more the Arab took his seat on the drooping donkey and the tiny procession came forward again. When they were directly under The Paralysed One, the mounted Arab looked up and gestured for the gate to be opened, at the same time patting the burden before him.

The legionnaire turned and looked down and saw that the commander of the fortress, Captain Jules Paon, had risen from his bed and was waiting below. With him were his lieutenants, *Le Gros* and *L'Irrité*. They had other names, but these were the names given them by their men, and they were better than those of their fathers. Putôt turned further, so that his good eye could survey the whole square. Everyone had turned out and was standing quietly below, even The Trinity . . .

The legionnaire twisted open his mouth and called down that there were Arabs outside, a party of three, who wished to come into the fort. They had with them, he said, a parcel, but he did not say what he considered to be inside that parcel, though he felt he knew.

Captain Paon, who was named the peacock but was drab as a peahen, jerked his craggy head towards the gate. At once

6

Sergeant Wilhelm Glik, who gave orders with a Latvian accent, roared out a command that the gate should be opened, and in the same breath cursed because it was not already done. He was the most feared of The Trinity, that name given to their three sergeants: Glik with his champing snapping teeth of stainless steel that were screwed into his jaws; Zirko the Swiss, with bad teeth, bad breath, and evil in his heart for all men; and Etienne Phare, who cursed men and beat them and shouted the name of God while he did so.

Those men nearest sprang to the baulks of timber that barred the great gate; they were as they had risen from siesta, nearly naked, but what did that matter in a desert outpost a hundred miles or more from the nearest place that might be given the label of civilisation?

The gate swung slowly open, groaning as its weight turned on the massive hinges. Framed in the entrance were the Arabs and their donkey. They did not approach at first, and their quick-moving brown eyes told of their suspicions

— their bodies were stiff and strained and ready for precipitate flight at the first sign of danger, but none came.

Only an invitation in guttural Arabic from Captain Paon to enter; it was the Arabic that he had learned in campaigns in Syria and the Lebanon, but it was understood — '*Taal-a-hone.*' Reassured, the mounted Arab kicked his bare heels into the protruding ribs of the donkey and the little party came through the gate. Just inside, once again they halted.

There was a stir among the men, a whisper that ran like a gentle summer breeze through a field of wheat. And then there was silence, and every man's eyes were fixed on that coarse-sacking bundle on the donkey's back.

Something unclean had crept into the air, polluting it, a stink that had been smelled before by these men under similar circumstances. Away on the west wall a sentry was slowly lifting his rifle and pointing it at the mounted Arab.

Captain Paon, an old man as officers went in the Legion, thin, stick-like legs astride, returned the salute that the Arabs gave him. The mounted Arab was fumbling inside the sack, and Paon gnawed his ragged moustache with impatience and then shouted to him to be quicker in whatever he was doing, though he, too, knew why the Arabs were here.

It came out. Something that seemed not much bigger than a grapefruit. The Arab casually tossed it across to the feet of the commanding officer.

It was a head.

Now, something happens to a head that has been hacked from its body. In the first place it grows small, so small that you cannot believe it to be anything but a child's. Secondly, the blood floods away leaving features, however tanned by subtropical suns, as delicately white as my lady's ungloved fingers . . . in time it will go yellow, of course, but in those first hours it has this pallor.

This head had fallen so that the men on the catwalks could look down upon the shrunken features — it lay with its hair curiously long, and coarse and black against the near-white sand. And men

9

hissed through their teeth as they saw that face. It was the face of a man who must have screamed for death. Those eyes were rolled up in torment, the bloodless lips drawn back from wide-bared teeth. He had died, but death could not have come soon enough for the man who had once had that face.

The safety catch clicked; the sights covered the rag that turbaned the head of the mounted Arab. The commanding officer moved. He was stiff, seeming elderly, though he was not as old as he looked; but tropical fevers in Madagascar and campaigns in the Near East had drained him of his vigour long ago. But his mind still held its sharpness, and the significance of that distant little sound was not lost on him.

His eyes, yellowed where whites once showed, came up; then his stick was pointing and his voice crackled, 'Fire, and you die against a wall today!'

The sentry slowly lowered his rifle. The other legionnaires shuffled and muttered, crowded there on the tiny parade square.

The Arab lost most of his apprehension

now, and his mobile face broke into a grin. He became even a little cocky, so sure of his safety.

It was, he was thinking, as the French said: an Arab would not be harmed if he came on such a mission. Now his fingers itched greedily to have hold of the promised reward. He spoke his mind in swift Arabic.

Captain Paon came blinking round into the sun again regarding that contorted face in the sand. He was uncertain. This could be anyone's head. He did not speak, but his face said so, and at that the Arab went into the sack and he pulled on something awkward in length inside. It came out and joined the head in the sand

It was a leg, naked, severed just as brutally from the body as that head. When they saw it, those legionnaires knew that little Pierre Planche would never again weep for his home in Provence. And he had been a good boy

Pierre, only silly in running away from his parents because someone had filled his head with stories that had made the Foreign Legion seem glamorous.

For there were unmistakable indications of ownership about that thin white leg, gleaming there in the hot, late afternoon sunshine. There were tattoo marks that had been made after enlistment in Marseilles, when the adventure seemed good to the country boy — not marks which can suitably be described here, but the kind that a giggling, drunken young fellow might request without heed to a future which would surely contain a wife for him

Unmistakably that was the leg of Petit Pierre; now without doubt, that was his head.

. . . Pierre who was too slow in his mind to keep ahead of the steel-toothed Latvian Glik, and who had suffered until he could suffer no more and had gone from his post at the gate one night last week. Now he had returned — two identifiable pieces of him.

Captain Paon nodded abruptly, satisfied. The Arab slipped off his donkey and came forward eagerly hand outstretched. Paon drew back in involuntary disgust then gave an order to Le Gros to pay the man his reward for bringing in a deserter. It was done, and in a few moments the Arabs had turned and were going quickly back down the trail, and the door was slammed shut after them, for not all Arabs came to El Zeeb with such little hostile intent.

And then the commander spoke to them as they stood there. He said that this should be an example to all men who harboured thoughts of desertion in their hearts. This man had betrayed his duty and had deserved to die.

'But not like that,' men thought to themselves. Not in such a way. Not to be tortured first by the Arabs who had found him alone in that great, hostile desert. For look at that face — didn't that speak of torment, awful and sustained? And all men's eyes were bitter and hating as they listened to that dried, spare stick of a commanding officer. For did they not all contemplate desertion at some time or other?

Captain Paon's harsh voice went on . . . But if there were men so base, so foolish, they must see that desertion was in any event not to be considered. Where could a man go in his madness? There was this desert all around, with not a growing thing, not a drop of water, for a hundred miles in every direction — not, that is, without an Arab watching over it.

He lifted his skinny wrists and gestured helplessly. And these Arabs — did they not see what happened when a man fell into their hands? Was such a fate to be considered? No, if any man had such thoughts, this must surely wipe them away.

Then he gave an order for the head and limb to be taken away, and he stood back and watched, stick tapping a leg that would look as thin and bloodless as Legionnaire Planche's, shortly.

2

The Opening of the Gate

Glik's voice roared in echo at the commander's order. Even before Captain Paon had finished speaking, Sergeant Glik was shouting.

'You and you, get this carrion away immediately. *Vitement!* Did you not hear me? Quickly, quickly!' Roaring so that the men indicated grew frantic in their haste to execute the unpleasant task.

And Glik kicked the head like a football between them as they came rushing up, and then shouted in anger because one had to turn and go back for it.

That was the way of Sergeant Glik. For it is a brutal, callous degrading thing to treat a poor man's head in such manner, and only a brutal, callous and degraded man could do it. And Glik wanted all to know that he was a brutal man and callous, even though it never occurred to

15

him that to be such was also to be degraded. Not that such a thought would have affected his conduct, in any event.

There were comforts in the legion if you were particularly brutal. For they quickly made you sergeant, and life was easier if you gave orders instead of taking them. With that simple idea in mind, from the first Sergeant Glik had been more brutal than the brutal, more callous than the most hardened. So, they had made him a sergeant.

Then the men went back to their beds in the stifling hot barrack rooms, to sit and talk, and curse and hate Authority above them. It was always so, after a deserter was brought in; it jangled men's nerves and made them unsettled and touchy and quarrelsome. Only a few seemed undisturbed — a few like le Legionnaire Gultos, who was slight and fair and was most usually known as *La Femme*, and Jacques Ficelle, and the yellow-toothed Second-class Legionnaire Marcel Corroyer.

But then Andre Gultos had had to leave Belgium in a hurry, and though joining the Legion had kept his neck as he preferred it, there was the disadvantage that it deprived him of that new-found thrill . . . But there are no small and helpless children in the Legion, upon whom a man might experiment at leisure. That was the Belgian known as *La Femme*.

Ficelle — he felt nothing except apprehension when his own safety was concerned. He had been a beater of women in Paris — a certain kind of woman, who is often beaten by a certain kind of man in order to make them share the money they came by so easily. The trouble was, he took to beating one frail little girl too zealously and she had died and — well, there he was in the Legion.

And Corroyer — as he has been mentioned, he, too, might as well be described. He was like a corpse — *une cadavre*, as Willi the Swiss would say — a doughy, unemotional creature who held a perpetual quality of being rankly unclean. He had no past, that anyone knew, but he was shunned because you cannot feel attracted towards some

17

thing that reminds you of sewers and untended drains, and perhaps being shunned divorced him from any feeling of warmth towards his fellow men.

For the rest, whatever their sins and crimes and faults, they were stirred by the end of their boy comrade, and they muttered together and walked restlessly up and down the bare barrack room and did angry things with their equipment.

And upon the ramparts, The Paralysed One lifted his rifle and covered the retreating Arabs and prayed that he could find a good reason for cracking open their skulls. But his prayer went without answer, and finally the exultant little party dropped out of sight just where the angry red sun would also disappear in two hours' time. Then, and only then, did he put down his rifle.

Dusk came, the short evening of the Sahara before the blackness of a moonless night. The guard was changed, the flag run down. Tonight would be hot and oppressive, and men would sleep badly, and perhaps some would have nightmares.

About midnight something unusual happened. The Englishman, Peter Warr, saw it all from his position on the catwalk above the gate where The Paralysed One had been posted earlier.

He wasn't mad, and yet he wasn't as other men. He had joined the Legion for no other reason than that he had wanted to.

He was tall and bony, with blue eyes that were quick and bright and held in them something not usual in men's eyes. It was too mild to warrant the title of fanaticism, but it promised that here was a man who would do quaint and crazy things and yet not see them as quaint and crazy at all.

He had no friends, Peter Warr, but he was friendly with everyone; he never seemed to need companions and curiously no one ever sought his company. He had an endurance far beyond normal men and seemed almost immune to the hardship and suffering that is the common lot among legionnaires — and for an Englishman he was remarkably oblivious to filth and flies and heat and ill-fitting uniforms . . .

Definitely not a normal English volunteer.

About eleven, with the sky soft and blue-black and stippled only with stars, suddenly Captain Paon came out from the centre block. He left the door open, so that the bright oil lamp inside his office seemed to light up the parade ground brilliantly, then he stood, slightly stooping, flicking that leg that he was so soon to lose, waiting for something.

The officer whom the men called The Irritable came out a few minutes later, and joined his commanding officer. They stood together for a few seconds in silence, L'Irrité turning his head quickly this way and that, as if looking for something to rouse his querulous temper.

After a time Captain Paon looked at his watch, and then called softly to the guardroom, '*Caporal!*'

Out came the corporal — running, stamping, saluting. Paon waved his hand with a quick little motion, as if requesting him to tone down his military zeal. Then he gave an order, indicating the English legionnaire above the gate.

The corporal started to shout. Captain Paon ripped out an order, quieted him, so that Legionnaire Warr only just understood when this time the corporal called up to him. Warr came down quickly, and was then told to help the corporal unbar the great gate. The locks undone, and the great timbers slid back, Warr naturally took hold of the gate to open it, but a sharp word from Captain Paon stayed the motion. The corporal and the legionnaire were then told to stand back a few yards, away from the gate, while Captain Paon and his lieutenant stood before it, waiting.

There was a silence over the fort, a silence broken only by the slight stirring of other sentries, high up at their posts on the walk, furtively watching when all their attention should have been directed outwards, across the dark desert.

Minutes passed — ten, twenty, half an hour. Paon never seemed to move, standing there in the yellow glow from the office light; his head drooped but his eyes never left that massive gate. In contrast L'Irrité fidgeted and moved from one leg to another and pulled out his handker-chief and then stuffed it back without doing anything with it.

Thirty-five minutes . . . There was an air about the waiting men, as if something dramatic was about to happen.

Warr's interested, blue eyes suddenly became attracted towards the gate. His mouth was slightly agape, showing the blackness where two front teeth had been; he looked scrawny, ridiculous, in the light that yellowed this end of the parade ground.

The gate began to swing slowly open.

Warr heard the corporal at his side suck in his breath, and then in an instant of panic the N.C.O. began to jump forward. L'Irrité caught the movement and flung up a quick, nervous hand in a gesture that halted the corporal.

Then they all stood and watched that gate as it crept slowly open — Paon, like a stiff old question-mark in the full beam of the office lamp; L'Irrité playing in quick movements with his stick; the corporal, swarthy, suspicious uneasy — his eyes so wide that the whites were complete rings round the molten brown centres. And Warr — tall and scraggy and interested in the way that a child is interested in the unusual.

Up on the catwalks those who could see but should not have been looking, were down on their knees, safety catches off, rifles pointing — and fingers ready to take the pressure of their triggers.

And nothing happened. When it was a yard open, the gate ceased to move further. They saw Captain Paon looking; he seemed to listen. Twice he nodded slowly. And then it was all over, and the gate slowly closed.

When it was shut, the fortress commander stood for a moment with his head on his chest, as if thinking and his thoughts were troubled. Then he stirred and waved his stick at the gate as an order to the corporal to bar it again, and then he turned and went stiff-legged up the outer step that led to his quarters atop the centre block. L'Irrité fluttered around vaguely for a moment, then went into the office and the light went off the parade ground as the door swung to.

The corporal and the legionnaire looked at each other as they swung the timbers across the gate. Then the corporal growled that it was no concern of his — 'Cela ne me regarde pas' and he said it quickly, moving his hands in impatient gestures, as if he washed his hands of the whole incredible affair. And then, because he was worried by the unusualness of it all, because he sensed that it could only presage trouble, he decided to get angry with the Legionnaire Warr, and he shouted to him to get up at his post what was he hanging around for?

If you cannot become a sergeant in the Legion, then second best is to be a corporal . . . but never a poor legionnaire!

When the legionnaire scrambled back to his post high above the arched gateway, there was nothing to see in the blackness that hung over the desert, nothing to indicate the origin of the night's mysterious affair. And so the night passed.

All too soon there was the sun again, the light that came hot and hurting to the eyes, the cloud of flies that wouldn't leave a man alone. But this day there was no wind, and the arid outlook was unbroken by the movement of man, beast or dust devils.

Yet the day was different. Everyone knew that away in the foothills the Arabs were massing for yet another revolt. How did they know? — no one had been outside the fort for days, and no one, except the Arabs who had brought back parts of poor Pierre Planche yesterday, had entered the fortress, and neither the Arabs nor Pierre could have given such information.

And yet every man in the fortress knew of it, knew that an oppressed and embittered tribe was gathering for yet another assault upon the representatives of the power that so unwisely governed them. And those representatives were themselves, the garrison of the Fortress El Zeeb.

Probably the rumour came from the officer's quarters, starting as a whisper into the big ears of some legionnaire servant and coming amplified to the men through his even bigger mouth.

Yet again, how did the officers come to

know? If they were the start of the rumour, that is? They hadn't been outside either . . .

Yet another incident occurred that was unusual that morning — actually it was an omission rather than an occurrence.

For the fort commander, Captain Paon, failed to appear on morning parade.

Such an event was unheard of, and caused consternation in the officers' quarters when the captain's servant reported the door locked and no answer to his calls from within. And it made the sergeants look blankly at each other, and they had to shout even louder than usual before they quieted the whispering from the men.

After the parade was dismissed and men were set to their duties that air of expectancy persisted and even grew, so that in time it produced an impossible atmosphere; and when it was more than curiosity could bear, men began to find reason for coming out on to the parade ground until by nine o'clock there wasn't a man absent from it.

They stood there, still and quiet, faces looking blankly upwards at the two lieutenants shouting through the door of the captain's quarters. It was all right for some to say that the captain was sleeping long after the mysterious affair of the night, of which all men knew by now, but no one was convinced.

A man does not sleep thus when there are others shouting through the keyhole at him, not a light-sleeping soldier like Captain Paon.

Le Gros made a decision. That could be said of him, big, sloppy and indolent though he had grown — he could make decisions. L'Irrité, now, he wasn't like that. He was indecisive, never certain, sure before he started that what he was doing would be wrong.

Le Gros adjusted those unmilitary-looking gold-rimmed pince-nez on his fat nose and barked out an order to Sergeant Glik. Steel teeth reflected light as the Latvian came jumping and shouting towards the men.

Two men would get bars and axes immediately — thou and thou. The others, in the name of heaven and certain other places, assuredly they would go back to their duties or they would inherit trouble. Yet after the first shuffle of feet, no one left the parade ground, and the sergeant was too concerned with other interesting matters to pay heed to them just then.

Captain Paon's quarters were in the square tower that lifted out of the centre block that stood just within the great wall to the north end of the fortress. There was only one entrance, and that gained by an open flight of broad, stone steps that ran up the outside of the tower.

The men came running up the steps with an axe and a long, chisel-ended steel bar. They looked doubtfully at the solid door that barred the way to the sacred quarters of their commander, but Le Gros waved a pudgy hand imperatively and ordered, 'Break it down!' Le Gros was fat but he had courage and when he gave orders there was no questioning them.

It was the Swiss legionnaire, Willi Pretel, who had the honour of knocking the door down. He lifted the axe, hefted it for a moment, and then swung it with a smash that sounded like an explosion in the stillness. The lock seemed to jump off the door as the axe bit into the wood above it; two more blows from that swinging axe and there was no need for the long lever.

Willi put his shoulder to the door and forced it back, and then went in. Le Gros called him out immediately, but it was too late. Willi had seen.

Le Gros went in, followed by L'Irrité and two of the sergeants. Then Glik was sent out to drive the men back to their work, and he did it to the accompaniment of so many kicks and curses that everyone knew that something extraordinary had happened inside the tower.

Willi came down with the axe. He was a big, quiet man, but the legionnaires would have none of his quietness now. They got him when he was round the corner and they kept him against the wall of the centre block until he had told them what he had seen up in the tower.

Willi told them. Captain Paon was

there — all of him. Only, his head was on the table, his right leg, as naked as Pierre's yesterday, was in a corner, while the rest of him slept a long last sleep in bed.

3

The Tower with the Tricolour

If you had stood outside Fortress El Zeeb that morning you would have heard a buzzing like a giant beehive. For a time, until The Trinity came shouting at the men, they stood in groups and speculated — and some said viciously they were glad; all officers were swine and deserved what came to them.

But there is a logical progression even to rumour. First it exhausts the subject as it is known to them, and then speculation goes beyond facts. In this case, within minutes the question on everyone's lips was: 'Who did it?'

Because no man can detach himself from his head and limb in such manner without assistance.

Who, then, had chopped the sleeping captain's head off, and butchered away a limb? Who? Who? Who? The question was on everyone's lips, from Le Gros down to the yellow-faced, scavenger-breathed Marcel Corroyer. Who among them had murdered the captain?

Strange, but no one asked, 'Why was it done?' Because in the Legion every man in time collects some reason for bearing a grudge against his commanding officer. And no one, come to that, was heard to declare indignantly against the murderer.

On the contrary. That was the man's own private affair, whoever it was. If he felt like that, if he had such a grievance that he must decapitate the captain, well . . . and everyone shrugged.

Perhaps not all. Not the officers; and sound, steady men like Willi Pretel, the Norwegian Odd Skadshaim, the long-moustached Joseph Tillfru who came from Austria, and the former Paris guttersnipe, Albert Volin, who had a heart of gold and who loved his uniform because it was the best suit of clothes he had ever worn — men like these were shocked and saddened by the brutality, though they did not speak against it. That would have meant to be laughed at, in that collection of hardened, desperate men.

Jacques Ficette loved it all, of course, and the slender girlish-figured legionnaire who had come to be called *La Femme* made a nuisance of himself by questioning the Swiss, Willi Pretel, getting him to go over and over again the picture as he had seen it. Until suddenly Fretel understood what was wrong with the man and said, irately, contemptuously, '*Sadiste!*' and pushed him roughly away.

He and Skadshaim, the Norwegian, were friends. Perhaps those snow-clad mountains back where their homes had been had given them something temperamentally in common and so they could feel at ease with each other, relaxed and trusting, as friends should be.

Willi lay on his bed with his heavy, ill-fitting boots overhanging the palliasse so as not to dirty it. He spoke quietly to his good friend the Norwegian.

'It was a bad thing to do, in imitation of what the Arabs did to poor little Pierre.'

That was what the whole garrison was talking about now — the fact that the murderer had deliberately mutilated his victim in exactly the same manner as the Arabs with the little deserter.

The big Swiss was genuinely shocked; his black-browed, low-voiced friend less so.

Odd Skadshaim reclined on the edge of the bed, his tunic unbuttoned at the neck. His grey eyes searched the barrack room from under his heavy eyebrows. He was a practical man, the Norwegian. He said, 'Whoever did it might be in this room.'

At that the Swiss sat up. He hadn't thought so far yet; perhaps he hadn't wanted to. His face was depressed and troubled as he looked at his comrades, talking in groups around the beds. He shook his head. 'I hope not.'

The phlegmatic Norwegian shrugged. 'Why? If he's not in this room, it's still some man we know equally as well; the murderer must be in this fortress, so he's a comrade of ours. Now, I wonder who it could be?'

He looked at Legionnaire Chopin, who bore an illustrious name but was distinguished in the legion only by his ability to thieve successfully. Chopin — there wasn't enough man in him to commit murder, the Norwegian thought. There was Fiertel, the German, who had bullied this room until unexpectedly a quite small man had risen in revolt and somehow defeated him in fair fight. Now, Fiertel could have done it; he had felt the lash of Captain Paon's tongue many a time and was brutal enough for any conduct.

The Norwegian looked at others — Tissdan, Schweld, Francois Delpage and Le Groneau. Rogues, rascals, vindictive and ill-tempered, treacherous — relishing brutality at any time, and always there to promote it when opportunity offered. Any of them would be capable of murder and of the excesses that had followed.

The only puzzling thing was that as the hours went by it began to appear impossible for a murder to have been committed at all.

That's what Lieutenant L'Irrité declared, when he and Le Gros had completed their examination. 'How could it have happened?'

His hands came up in quick, jerky gestures, embracing the door and the windows in turn. 'The door was locked and one bolt shot across from the inside; there is a thirty-foot drop from these windows.'

Le Gros adjusted those silly gold-rimmed pince-nez glasses and said with his customary roughness, 'Well, it did happen, didn't it? Do you think Paon did this to himself?' He didn't say, 'You fool,' but his manner implied it. He was a soft, bloated, fleshy man, but there was nothing soft about his speech.

He stood at the window. It was big enough for a man to have entered by it, and it had been found wide open when they came into the room. The centre block, on which this tower was built, was completely detached from the fortress wall, the idea being that if attack breeched the outer defence, the garrison might retire into the centre block and continue their resistance.

The fortress wall was lower than the window, permitting a view across the desert to those distant foothills where Arab tribesmen were gathering for assault on the post. It was also some twenty feet away, with a thirty-foot drop to the ground below. A fly could have climbed those smooth walls; a man, no.

Le Gros looked at that wide-open window and said, 'The assassin must have come this way. *Le capitaine* would never have slept with a window so wide open as this.'

It seemed to be reasonable, that theory; the only thing against it was — how had the murderer bridged that twenty-foot gap? For there would also be a sentry continually pacing the catwalk immediately below.

Le Gros found Zirko of the bad teeth at his elbow and said, 'I wish to question last night's guard. Parade them at once.' The sergeant saluted and went off with a fine show of military zeal.

Lieutenant L'Irrité was out of humour by now and started to speak peevishly. 'I do not understand anything about this affair, Anton. Nothing, I tell you. I am bewildered. It is beyond my comprehension.' He was getting worked up and his hands were talking faster than his mouth, his shoulders shrugging not much slower. He was an unhappy man, Lieutenant L'Irrité; he was never meant for a commanding position over men and he knew it yet didn't have strength enough to pursue reason to a logical conclusion. And so he lived a life of continual worry and unhappiness.

Le Gros ignored him. That was Le Gros. He was ponderously sure of himself . . .

L'Irrité in vexation started to tap the steel ladder out in the hall that gave access through a trapdoor to the walled, flat-topped roof of the tower — a commanding position in time of attack. Le Gros spoke heavily, massively — 'Control yourself, Armaund. An officer must never show uncertainty before the men and we must face them now.'

He didn't mean to offer insult to the junior lieutenant, but it was always there, in his manner — a condescension, a contempt, even. L'Irrité blinked down at the floor and wished that that was Le Gros's fat head on the table and not Paon's. Paon was so distant that he never bruised the lieutenant's feeling; Le Gros was so close always that he couldn't avoid his unconscious barbs of speech.

As the two officers descended the stone steps, Sergeant Etienne Phare came in sight, bringing up a small party at the double. They were to box their commanding officer together; later that morning there would be a burial. Bodies didn't keep in that heat.

It was appropriate that Sergeant Phare should have charge of the funeral proceedings, for Sergeant Phare was a man of God. Only his god wasn't the god of other men.

He was a small, shrunken man, with a small, shrunken face, but his eyes were big and they had fires in them always, as if the owner were in an advanced stage of malaria. He had a belief, this soldier, old in the service of France, a belief that poured in a high hot stream from his toothless, gummy mouth every waking hour of the day — a belief in the divine right of those born to command.

Etienne Phare believed that those in

39

authority were gifted by God; accordingly, any act of opposition to Authority, even to the lowest of corporals, was a flouting of God's wishes, to be punished suitably. And Sergeant Etienne Phare was in true lineal descent of the Inquisitors when it came to meting out punishment to the deserving.

He was the most rigid disciplinarian; if he gave an order it had to be obeyed down to the very last letter. And if it were not, or if he thought it insufficiently carried out, Sergeant Etienne Phare would jump in, eyes aflame as men's eyes must have flared with holy zeal in times when they broke men on the rack or enclosed them in the coffin of spikes ... Only Phare used his fists and his heavy boots, and while he made the blood run his voice shouted to heaven to witness the justness of the punishment that was being inflicted.

The sergeant's name was Phare, which means beacon or lighthouse. It is doubtful if that was his real name.

His first act was to lower the tricolour to half-mast. It was a proud splash of

40

colour against the brilliant African sky, and it seemed to come reluctantly down the mast that reared from the west corner of the towers.

Phare performed the ceremony himself. He liked ceremonies; and wasn't he God's servant and so fitted to perform it adequately? He stood on the small platform atop the stone steps and carefully fastened the cords to the peg on the wall. Then he stood back and saluted, while the other legionnaires watched with eyes lowered to hide their contempt. They could not share all the pride in their sergeant's heart — perhaps there were too many of them, just then.

Having performed the lowering of the flag ceremony, they went into the death chamber. It was simple work — one man to clean and burnish the late captain's sword that had performed the butchery; the others to assemble him inside his best uniform, so that when he lay in the long, dough-sided box he looked not unlike a whole man.

Except that his head was so very curiously small, as Pierre Planche's had looked, only yesterday out there on the parade ground.

Then they took him and buried him on a mound just outside the fort, and built a cairn to keep away animals, and topped it with a wooden cross that disappeared within days, for wood is a valuable commodity in a desert that bears no trees. Why should the dead have it, when poor Arabs had better use for it?

But before this, before the funeral procession and firing party, many things happened.

Le Gros was a good soldier. This act must be reported at once to the battalion HQ at Alfia on the coast; there was also the intelligence received about a serious massing of Arab malcontents who proposed to destroy this isolated fortress of El Zeeb.

A corporal and two legionnaires were despatched. Each carried a copy of the lieutenant's report; each was told to get through at all costs. Light men were picked, men who would not tire a horse rapidly; and they were given the finest horses in the small stable — the corporal, as an example, was mounted on the late Captain Paon's small, proud, glossy-black Arab steed.

They trotted out of the fort and westward along the dusky trail, a dust cloud rising and lingering to a height of about two or three feet as they passed. They had a hundred miles to go, and no possibility of a change of mounts. They would canter steadily as long as possible, and only use their spurs if they came across hostile Arabs.

Last night's guard was paraded, and Le Gros and L'Irrité came down to question them. Two men had shared the duties of sentry on the catwalk immediately behind and below that open window of the captain's quarters.

No, they said, they had heard nothing unusual. No one had entered or left by that window while they were on duty. And their expressions said, 'How could they? Have men wings or the ability to jump higher than cats — far higher?'

On consideration the last sentry on duty before reveille remembered that a light had come on in the captain's quarters. He also remembered the sound of movement from within, but he had thought at the time that it might be *le capitaine* preparing early for the day's duties. Yes, he remembered hearing the window being opened — that was just after the light had gone out inside the room. No, it was not possible to see within the captain's room from that position atop the catwalk; the window was too high above them.

Le Gros watched their faces closely while they spoke. He was thinking, 'The assassin killed Paon, then lit the lamp the better to see what he was doing. When he had performed his vile atrocities, he put out the lamp, then opened the window . . . and escaped.'

But how, unless these men were lying? How could he have entered and escaped by that window, with a twenty-foot gap, a thirty-foot drop, and a legionnaire on duty immediately outside? It didn't make sense.

He thought again, starting from the beginning, because Le Gros was no slouch mentally, though lazy when it came to any exercise except eating and drinking.

The door had been locked from within. The only possible entry could have been made by one or other of the windows . . . He remembered the steel ladder and the trapdoor leading to the flat roof. That was a possible way in, also, if a man were a bird and able to fly.

He grew annoyed, because he was baffled. For if a man could gain the roof and so make use of the internal ladder into the captain's quarters, then it seemed to him that he could the more easily gain that window part way up the tower.

No, no, he thought; that window was the clue to the whole affair. It was so wide open, obviously there was significance behind it; clearly the murderer must have used it.

But then it didn't make sense. Not with a sentry right outside.

So Le Gros stuck his silly gold-rimmed spectacles on to the end of his fat nose and roughly told the pair they were lying and he would tear the truth out of them. Clearly they were lying. Mon dieu, did they realise what a story they were telling him?

They were saying that a miscreant could enter and leave by a window right under their very noses and they would never see it. He made an expression of disgust at their foolishness. Clearly the assassin had placed *une planche* or a ladder across from the top of the wall so that it rested on the window ledge of the captain's quarters. Could that have happened if they had been awake?

Or, and Le Gros waited suitably so that the accusation could hit them the harder when it came — *or, were they not accomplices if not the assassins themselves.*

The men protested. They were startled, frightened by the unexpectedness of the situation. Suddenly horrified by the danger that faced them. They were Frenchmen, simple men from the industrial Rhine valley; what they were doing in the Legion neither they nor anyone else knew. But they were here, and now — this.

Le Gros tried to stampede them into a

confession of guilt; if not, at least he hoped he could make them let fall some indication of their complicity in the affair. He stood over them, shouting. His hand was raised as though to strike them out of horror and indignation, though he never did. He shook the men, he threatened them with the penal battalions, with summary justice out here in the desert, with trial and a firing party for certain for them back at Alfia.

But neither broke down, terrified though they were, neither departed from his original story. If they were not telling the truth, at least they were consistent in their lying.

When he was tired of it, out there in the hot sun, Le Gros suddenly dismissed the parade, but ordered Sergeant Glik the Latvian to put the two sentries concerned in the punishment cells. They were rushed away to an accompaniment of blows and curses, and threats of the most incredible ferocity if they persisted in this obstinate attitude of keeping their mouths shut. Glik was sure if he could have the men for an hour, he would drag a confession out of them. Which is probably correct; men will confess to anything at times in order to end a torture.

After the guard parade was dismissed, the whole garrison with the exception of the wall guard paraded to give last honour to their late commander. He was buried. The new, if temporary commander, Le Gros, said that here lay a brave man, a man who had done his duty by his country and had been foully slain while still in active service. He said many other fine things too, but no man not even the generous Willi the Swiss shared his appreciation. For they had stood long, and the sun was fierce upon them, and anyway the commander to them represented all the brutality of their sordid existence. He had died; he was dead. Why say more about it? Why not get back to the shade of their barrack rooms, stifling hot though they were?

When, shortly after midday, that parade was dismissed, too, Le Gros climbed slowly up the steps to the captain's quarters. He was baffled by it all, but obstinacy made him carry on with the investigation. After all, he would look a fine successor to Paon if, when a relief came, they found he had been unable to detect the miscreant. He must find him; clearly that was what he must do.

So he went back into the death chamber, though his sluggish limbs cried out for the comfort of his bed and a siesta, and his throat wanted the bottle that could make him forget the drabness of this desert existence.

He crossed again to the window and looked out. Twenty feet away was the battlemented top of the fortress wall; rather below and keeping watch through an embrasure was a sentry. Le Gros sighed. It all seemed so incredible. Surely the murderer or murderers could only have crossed this gap and entered by this window with the complicity of one or other of the sentries? There could be no other explanation for it.

The explanation was simple, if a sentry were in on this. A ladder or a plank — *une planche*. Le Gros suddenly realised that that was the name of the legionnaire who had deserted and lost his

49

head and a leg in the process. Plank — *planche*. Perhaps it was symbolical in some way.

In any event, it was a murder of retribution. That was too apparent. Some friend of the dead deserter had ascribed the death to the commanding officer, and had killed him and mutilated him in exactly the same way out of revenge.

But who was the friend?

Le Gros found his attention attracted by a movement far out on the desert. It was a cloud of dust, and growing. Perhaps, he thought, it was some mounted Arab crossing to the hill villages. He suddenly had another thought.

It was Arabs who had killed and mutilated the legionnaire, these Arabs who were massing now to destroy the garrison. The way Paon had been treated was an Arab way, not a European's.

He found himself wondering if there wasn't something in the thought, wondering if Paon's death, like Planche's, wasn't of Arab origin. Then he dismissed the thought abruptly; for how could an Arab have scaled this wall last night and crossed over into Paon's quarters while sentries paced the wall outside?

'Ridiculous,' he thought impatiently, and yet the idea wouldn't leave him. He looked again at that distant cloud on the horizon, and it seemed as though it were growing larger, as if approaching.

Le Gros waddled into the tiny passageway that gave access to the broken, outer door. Inside the passage was the steel ladder that gave access to the roof. Le Gros sighed but started to climb. He felt uncomfortably hot, and sticky with sweat. All the same he wanted to see everything, because who knew what important clue might not be awaiting him around some corner, a clue that would unmistakably point out the identity of the wretched assassin?

The trapdoor was heavy, and he climbed close to it so that it lifted on his beefy shoulders and not on his head. As he climbed it rose and then finally fell with a bang on to the roof top. The heavy bolts were fitted atop the trap, because in case of final emergency the last stand would be made up here . . . bolts on the

51

inside of the trapdoor would accordingly have no value.

Le Gros sat on the edge of the trapdoor in order to recover his breath, and the noonday sun poured on him with sickening intensity. It was not long before he rose and crossed to the low defence parapet and looked out across the desert.

Above him, disconsolately at half-mast, the flag of France stirred for a moment and then drooped limply down again. Heat haze shimmered and distorted the view; Le Gros had to watch intently for several minutes before he was able to make out the approaching rider.

It was a legionnaire. One.

And three had just ridden out.

4

It was an Arab Assassin!

Le Gros turned and waddled hastily across to the trapdoor and started to go down. He felt uneasy, an unease brought on by sight of that solitary, hard-riding legionnaire. Just for a second, descending, he paused and looked up at the square of blue sky where the open trap gaped above him.

He thought, 'A man . . . an assassin . . . could get into the tower easily this way, because that trap doesn't bolt from the inside.'

But how could a man reach that rooftop, the highest point in the fortress, unless he could fly?

Le Gros clicked his tongue impatiently. What thoughts to have. Clearly the clue was contained in *une planche* — and that meant that one or both of those sentries was complicit in the crime if not actually the murderer himself. Well, he would drag the truth from the wretch somehow. Perhaps if Sergeant Glik were encouraged . . .

He washed quickly, in his quarters, and while he slopped the water over his head he spoke to L'Irrité. His voice kept rising in gasping gulps as he sluiced himself under the refreshing cold water, and it disgusted the junior lieutenant. This man was a pig, he thought, with the manners of a pig. Viciously he found himself wishing that he could see Le Gros' fat head on a table — it would be appropriate, for wasn't that how they treated pigs' heads?

It was a silly thought, a momentary viciousness that went as quickly as it came. But living with the gross Anton could be torment. Anton was insensitive, crude, untidy; L'Irrité was the opposite in all things.

L'Irrité was trying not to listen, trying to read a magazine that was many months old and had been read before. And Le Gros was talking to him, ranting on about this miscreant, whoever he was. L'Irrité thought, 'If I had to submit to the treatment of men like Paon and Le Gros, perhaps I too would have homicidal thoughts.' But then L'Irrité was not a good officer and was out of place in this Legion. Perhaps his parents might have done better to have apprenticed him to the church and not to an army.

Le Gros said, suddenly, 'Armaund, you are not listening.' He said it peremptorily, as if addressing someone of inferior intelligence and lesser age. He meant nothing by it; he didn't even realise that his manner was unpleasant and insulting. And so he was jerked into astonished erectness when L'Irrité hurled down his ancient magazine, bounded excitedly to his feet, and shouted, 'Oh, yes, I heard you. You have some new theory now, that an Arab climbed through that window and killed Captain Paon. You see, I heard you, didn't I?' And he rushed out, trembling with rage.

And someone else heard him. Those same big ears.

Le Gros recovered his breath, shrugged

his heavy shoulders, and simply forgot the incident.

He went out and gave orders for a man to climb up and shut the trap door in the commander's quarters, then went across to the main gate. The sentry had already called down to the corporal of the guard, who was directing the opening of the gate. He wheeled, saluting, as Le Gros dragged his weight across the square.

'*Qui est-il!*' demanded Le Gros.

'*C'est le caporal Brissel*,' said the guard commander.

'Brissel?' That was the corporal who had gone with the report to Alfia with two legionnaires. This was ominous.

The gate opened. Brissel was half a mile off, walking his horse in slowly. Both looked weary, but as they came near and the corporal made out Le Gros's bulk, he straightened himself and came the last distance at a slow trot.

He saluted, slid from his saddle, and made a brief report.

They had ridden steadily towards Alfia until about twelve miles out. Then they had come across a band of mounted

56

Arabs crossing the trail. The Arabs had turned in pursuit. The corporal had ordered his men to ride northwards in the hope that one would find a way through, while he had ridden across the face of the Arabs in the hope of creating a diversion. He was a brave man, that corporal.

Le Gros nodded his big head approvingly. 'And was the manoeuvre a success?'

The corporal sighed and shook his head. No. He had seen the two legionnaires run slap bang into a crowd of Arabs who had suddenly rode down a dry wadi into their path. He shrugged his shoulders to indicate what a limited life they would have after that.

And he — he had seen the way barred by an almost unbroken stream of Arabs riding in from the desert towards *la village negre*. There was no way through them, so he had wheeled his horse, outdistanced the Arabs who appeared to have come a long way and were riding tired beasts, and ridden for Fortress El Zeeb.

But he had more to tell. The failure of the expedition to get through to Alfia was nothing beside the threat of those massing Arabs. They were riding in thousands, he said, and his black, doleful eyes showed exaggerated concern. Assuredly this was a revolt on a big scale; if they attacked the fort, as rumour said they intended, then the garrison would be hard put to it to keep off those thousands of fanatical warriors.

When he had finished, all stood silently for a moment out there on the blistering desert. Then Le Gros said, '*Mon enfant,* you have brought credit to yourself,' and dismissed him. And then he dismissed thoughts of the Arab rising, because that was something the future contained; just now he was determined that his first act as fort commander would be to find the assassin of Captain Paon.

In the barrack rooms, where the next guard was busy preparing equipment and weapons for the afternoon mounting, there was a lot to talk about. There was also a lot to make men's sharp tempers rip open and show themselves; for it is no fun to be cooped inside a fortress for weeks on end, with endless, monotonous duties to follow, and little relief from the summer Sahara sun. That glare alone during a daylight spell on guard was sufficient to give a headache that would last until the next spell on duty — or so there were many to declare, anyway.

And the talk was of Arab vengeance.

Those big mouths from the officers' quarters had opened. Le Gros, they said, had a theory that perhaps the murderer or murderers of Captain Paon had come from outside. It was an act of Arab vengeance, those Arabs who were massing outside right now. First little Pierre Planche, and then, in same manner, the fort commander.

'And why?' It was Chopin, spreading those slim and useful fingers that were yet useless on a piano keyboard, and made him undeserving of the great name he bore by virtue of their propensity for sliding into people's pockets.

Chopin was excitable, and he liked to make everyone excited around him. He had decided to believe in this story of Arab vengeance and he was the kind of man who, believing, must see that others believed, too.

'Why was Paon killed? *Mes foi*, is it not apparent? Are you not dullards not to see it?' He grew warm in his contempt for the less perceiving.

Willi Pretel said, drily, '*Mais oui, mon ami*. We are dullards, are we not? Only the great, the intelligent Monsieur Chopin understands. Now, do tell us quickly what it all means and then close your wagging mouth. The room is warm enough without more hot air.'

Chopin pulled a face with exaggerated unconcern for one, Willi Pretels, opinion. He turned to more congenial company, remarking as he did so about the intolerable thickness of some people's skulls, especially those born in Switzerland. Willi Pretel grinned at his good friend, the black-browed Odd Skadshaim, and lay back on his bed and tried to forget for a moment that he was out here in a hell on earth while somewhere were tall mountains, and cool spring water running always down the sides, and a sun that was kind and caressed you, unlike this raging, hateful thing above them now.

Chopin was urging, trying to convince. Which was always the way with this propagandist. 'Don't you see, it's all bound up with this Arab rising. They want us to see that we are vulnerable; at any time they can reach out and pluck us off — like that!' He made the gesture of plucking off his head.

But he was alone in this theory; while the men were content to discuss and argue about the possibility of Arab responsibility for the latest killing, none really believed it none would accept it. For that matter, Chopin didn't really believe it, but the thought having occurred to him, he could not let it go but must insist that others shared it.

Hans Fiertel in the end shut him up. The man who had once been the bully of the barrack room called back some of his old power. He rolled on to his side on the bed and snarled, '*Gott in Himmel*, must you keep on with your talk?' And that shut the propagandist up, though with poor grace; for there was an expression on Fiertel's hard, shiny, formless face that promised a swift blow if he were not careful.

The sudden, savage snarl brought Willi Pretel's eyes round. Once Fiertel had been a nuisance in the barrack room, always bullying men and striking out for no reason other than that some N.C.O. or officer had bullied him and made him bad-tempered. Pretel hoped that he wasn't going to start with his tantrums again.

For the last few weeks he had been very subdued, and life had been accordingly so much the pleasanter.

Pretel's eyes lazily moved down the line of beds until they fell on Legionnaire Dalarge, he who had been the cause of Fiertel's discomfiture. It was still incredible, how it had happened.

Fiertel had been in trouble out on the parade ground. He had stormed back to the barrack room in a fury of anger, had picked on someone — Pretel couldn't even remember who, now — and started to kick him down the floor. When Fiertel was angry he had to hurt someone, and only the slightest pretext was needed to send his fists and feet lashing out at the unfortunate legionnaire. Because he was so strong, so vicious and ill-tempered, no one had really stood up to the bully until that particular day.

Then Dalarge had taken it upon himself to attack the hulking German. Dalarge wasn't anywhere near as tall — the German, nowhere near as strong — yet he suddenly catapulted himself off his bed and hurled himself on to the astonished Fiertel.

Perhaps the unexpectedness of the attack had helped Dalarge. Anyway, it wasn't a stand up fight in which Fiertel would surely have come off best; it was more like the frenzied ferocity of two tumbling cats, rolling over each other on the barrack room floor, fists and feet flailing so fast that the eye could hardly see them.

And it was all over in the space of a couple of minutes, though two minutes can seem a long time if you are fighting.

Dalarge fought like a madman, unheeding the blows that came in return. Fiertel started by bellowing with rage, then his roaring changed to gasps of pain . . . then as the rain of blows closed his eyes and tore his nose open and split his lips and turned his body into a mass of fiery bruises, he whimpered. When he was silent and still, Dalarge still went on battering him until Albert Volin, Joseph Tillfru and a few others dragged him off. Then he went quite quietly and sat himself down on his bed and gave his attention to his equipment once more.

He was a curious man, Dalarge. Pretel saw that he was in his accustomed place on the edge of his bed, fiddling around with something white. Stocky, swarthy, little Dalarge never seemed to rest like other men, always he was doing something, adjusting some equipment or fiddling around with a rifle or polishing something that no longer needed polishing because it was his. And Pretel knew that the unrest was more than physical; it lay deep underneath, too.

Dalarge hardly ever spoke, but he thought a lot, you could see that. His eyes which never smiled, told of quick, nervous thoughts, of a suppression that was bad for the owner . . .

Pretel saw that Dalarge was bandaging his hands — both of them.

Then he sat up, startled. For Fiertel was looking at those bandaged hands, and it wasn't hard to read what was going on in his mind.

Fiertel was thinking: *Dalarge has hurt his hands. Dalarge who humbled me and hurt me. And a man cannot fight his best when his hands are hurt.*

Fiertel was thinking sudden thoughts of revenge.

Pretel swung off his bed to warn Dalarge, then sat down again as Fiertel relaxed and stretched with his hands under his head. It seemed that the moment was over.

★ ★ ★

Across in the officers' quarters Le Gros was slowly draining a glass of almost neat liquor. When it was finished he made a slopping sound as he licked his lips, and that jarred the sensitive junior lieutenant. L'Irrité jerked his magazine (which he wasn't reading, though his eyes were following the lines of print) so that it cut out the sight of that big, sagging, over-fleshed form, as if that way it would exclude him from his senses, too.

Le Gros saw and understood the movement. It didn't worry him, because he couldn't feel that the fault — if there was a fault — was his. Of course poor Armaund was under the weather. With condescension, he thought what a poor soldier this man was, and how ill-fitted he had proved to be for his career as a soldier. This eternal sun and sand and desert hardship in a lonely post was proving too much for his nerves.

It didn't have the same effect on Le Gros. Of course he would have preferred the comforts of the coast town of Alfia, for there were charming ladies to provide diversion, while here there was only liquor. The loneliness of this desert post didn't seem to affect him much; when there was nothing to do he found it quite comfortable just to lie down and drink until sleep came. Yes, he thought, life was supportable even in El Zeeb if one had the fortitude of mind to approach the problem properly.

He said, 'You find my conduct disagreeable, Armaund?' There was no tact and delicacy about Le Gros, but to give him his due neither was there heat and anger. It was just a plain statement that he made.

L'Irrité sat and quivered behind his magazine, not saying anything, only wanting some of the peace that he could never find as an officer of the Foreign Legion. It was no use arguing with Le Gros because his brother officer was always so sure himself, and there is little profit in arguing with a man who knows he is right.

His silence failed to disturb Le Gros. He looked through his glasses at the slightly shivering magazine and said, 'Very well, Armaund. It is easy to resolve the problem. I annoy you with my conduct, therefore I will cease to annoy you.'

He rose, as if he had come to a decision. L'Irrité let fall the magazine, surprised. 'I do not understand,' he began, because he knew that Le Gros could no more change his annoying habits than the proverbial leopard could jump away from its spots.

Le Gros grinned slightly, pleased because he had roused his companion. 'I think I'll move into Captain Paon's quarters tonight,' he said dryly. 'Then you will be relieved of my obnoxious presence, *mon cher Armaund*.'

Actually, of course, the reason why he had decided on the move was because the tower was high and caught any breeze that crept across the desert, and at night it was especially cool and pleasant to be up there.

Startled, L'Irrité dropped his magazine. There was something indecent about moving so quickly into a dead man's bed, though as commander of El Zeeb Le Gros had a perfect right to, of course. As is the way with human flesh, of course, the objection L'Irrité raised was not this one, however.

He said, 'But is there not danger, Anton? After all, the murderer is at large; might he not strike again — at you?'

He was remembering his earlier thoughts, how he'd wished that it was Le Gros's fat head resting on that plain wood table, and somehow it made him feel guilty — as though that thought of his had inspired in Le Gros this contemplated action, which could possibly end in another tragedy.

Le Gros discovered that he could see better without his glasses than with them, so he removed them and started to polish them on his shirtfront. While he did so he spoke.

He talked calmly, too calmly, so that his voice seemed heavy and he seemed to be speaking down to L'Irrité.

'Danger? I see no danger. A murderer rarely strikes twice, for one thing, but, more important, I think I shall know the name of the miscreant before this evening.'

'You will?' L'Irrité's eyes were troubled. He didn't like the tone of that last remark. 'How?'

Le Gros carefully adjusted his spectacles on his formless potato of a nose, then said, 'I am going to the punishment cells now. I think one or the other will talk.' After a pause he gave what seemed sufficient reason for his statement. 'Sergeant Glik and I will ask a few questions.'

He went heavily out into the sunshine, leaving L'Irrité to feel suddenly sick. He was a bad officer, L'Irrité; too sensitive to be in the Foreign Legion. Instinctively he was opposed to this brutality that enforced discipline, yet curiously there were times when he shared in it himself.

Sometimes he found himself storming at men in unnecessarily savage manner; many times he had committed men to punishment though in his heart he knew they were undeserving. Then, afterwards, he would lie on his bed and hate himself; for he knew that what he had done was in reaction to all the things that hurt him in his life as an officer in this hated Foreign Legion.

Across the parade ground Le Gros saw Glik the Latvian. He lifted his hand in a gesture, saw the quick salute and the flash of light as the steel teeth were bared. Then Glik came doubling over, to stamp at attention before him.

Le Gros looked at that big hard face, burned nearly black by years in the

Legion, looked at those narrowed slits of eyes that showed no trace of softness for any man or anything. He found himself nodding. If he had had any doubts before, he had none now.

He said, 'You will accompany me to the punishment cells, sergeant. One or both of those men assisted in the murder of our commanding officer even if he — or they — did not perform the killing himself. You and I are going to find the truth of the matter, yes?'

He was watching the big Latvian while he spoke, and now he saw that big hard face soften, the eyes relax and open a little. Then a tongue came from between those parallel rows of gleaming steel and licked thin lips.

Sergeant Glik knew what was expected of him. Sergeant Glik was prepared to give full and overflowing measure.

5

Stand to!

They knew in the barrack rooms before the pair were through the door of the punishment cell block. Tissdan, the German slipped in and made the announcement. 'Le Gros has gone to interrogate the prisoners. Sergeant Glik is with him.'

That woke them up. The presence of Sergeant Glik could mean only one thing.

Men sat on their beds, heads drooping, waiting and listening; for they knew that when they came they would hear the sounds from the punishment cells.

After a time they heard Glik's thick voice roaring, then a man cried out in pain. After that the cries were more frequent, sometimes rising into a scream.

It unnerved men, sitting there help-lessly waiting and listening. It could so easily have been one of them, each man

72

was thinking; right now it might have been them in that small, bare cell, with Sergeant Glik striking them and performing unmentionable cruelties in order to get them to talk.

They wanted noise, to keep out the sounds, but something kept them quiet so that they could hear everything.

All, that is, except the girlish La Femme, who listened intently, straining lest he missed a quaver from that tortured screaming voice ... La Femme who could enjoy doing terrible things, as he had once done back in his native Belgium. And Ficelle sometimes grinned to himself when the shriek came up quickly, as though it amused him and he found something comical about the cry. And Corroyer didn't seem to mind, didn't seem even to hear it. He put his scrubby, unwashed head onto his dirty pillow and went to sleep.

Little Albert Volin, who should have had no fine feelings because of his origins, at length could stand it no longer. He got to his feet and began to pace the room, rapidly and nervously, and as he walked he shouted, '*Mon dieu*, that men should do such things to men!' And he swore that there was no God, or assuredly he would not permit such wickedness.

Willi Pretel said, 'You must calm yourself, Albert. It is wicked, just as you say, but what can we do about it? Remember, we are legionnaires in the Foreign Legion, and this is all part of our lot.'

'Justice,' shouted little Albert. 'That's what we need. Do you hear me? It is time there was justice, at least in this wretched *Legion Étrangers*.'

Men murmured at that, in approval of what he said. And Pretel saw a curious expression in the eyes of Legionnaire Sebastian Dalarge, he of the bandaged hands.

In some way all this excited the German Fiertel, too; it quickened his pulse and made him want to do something. Only, being Legionnaire Fiertel doing something meant violent physical exercise. He had had too little since that thrashing he had received so unexpectedly and unaccountably, and he was long since recovered of the bruises.

Now he shouted to Volin to shut his mouth; did the whole barrack room want to hear his yapping? He said it in his old manner, not because the noise assailed him but because he was up to his old games of seeking excuse for action.

Volin, lulled by these recent weeks of quietness on the part of the former bully, ignored him and went on with his stamping and declaiming against God and Heaven. Fiertel rose from his bed, working himself up into a rage.

'*Mein gott*,' he kept growling. 'You will learn the price of disobedience, my small friend.'

He grabbed Volin and ran him quickly against a wall. Skull and back smote against it with sickening force and poor little Albert Volin went white and his eyes grew dazed and his body was a weight on his aggressor's arms. Pretel was on his feet at once. But he was such a man of peace that he was as helpless as an old woman; always he sought to reason with men, not knowing that some men are removed from reasoning.

Odd Skadshaim the Norwegian knew it, however. He was a more direct man. He stamped to his feet, black brows contracting the hollows of his cheeks more than usually accentuated. But he kept his head, even in the midst of anger. He said to the hesitating Willi Pretel, 'It will need the pair of us, *mon ami*. Come, let us settle with him now.'

Willi nodded, recognising the truth of the statement; he stepped forward, though he hated the thought of having to strike a comrade, even under such circumstances.

But swarthy, stocky Legionnaire Sebastian Dalarge was there before them. Fiertel had slammed the unfortunate Albert Volin against the wall close by the head of Dalarge's bed. At once everyone in the room recognised that that had been no accident. Fiertel was hoping to provoke Dalarge into another assault. If he did, this time he, Fiertel, would not be taken by surprise; this time he would know how to handle the wild-cat legionnaire. He would drive him off and then kick him into insensibility — those were the tactics. And Dalarge wouldn't be able to do much with his hands because he had hurt them and they were bandaged.

Which latter situation contains the whole reason for Fiertel's sudden courage.

And Dalarge came rising from his bed in fierce anger.

'Justice,' some near by heard him say, and then he flung himself at the bully.

Fiertel let the little Albert slide to the ground and stepped back. Dalarge tried to shift his attack and turn to come in, but Fiertel drove one ponderous fist into his ear and smashed him against the wall on top of the feebly-stirring Albert. Then Fiertel came in, kicking.

Pretel hated physical violence, but he was a strong man, all the same. Fiertel suddenly found himself hefted and tossed on to Dalarge's bed. He sat up, face almost black with fury. 'I am attacked,' he called to his friends. '*Au secours!*'

In an instant the room was a camp divided against itself. Horowicz, Stephanie, Le Groneau, Tissdan, Schweld and half a dozen ranging themselves by the side of Fiertel — Joseph Tillfru, Selglas, and four or five like men rising to the aid of Willi Pretel and party. Dalarge staggered to his feet and would have hurled himself at the throat of the bigger, stronger Fiertel, only Pretel restrained him.

Tissdan came up suddenly, trying to swing at Pretel, but the silent Norwegian, Odd Skadshaim, just kicked him on the kneecap and sent him shouting with pain into a heap on the floor. That stopped the rush.

Pretel said, 'We thought you had learned your lesson, Fiertel. But if you haven't, perhaps we should teach it you now, yes?'

One moment later there would have been a savage battle in progress in that barrack room, with a very crowded block of punishment cells to house them afterwards; only two things happened in quick succession.

The first was a scream from the punishment cells, so swift and sudden that it arrested all motion inside that barrack room. It stopped all sound, too, so that plainly they heard its dying cadences and then the sobs that followed. A man sobbing. A man crying like a child. A man of the Foreign Legion. Truly he must have suffered at the hands of the Latvian to be reduced like that.

Pretel saw Lafarge's face before him. Those brown eyes burning. But it was little Albert Volin, staggering on to his feet again, who spoke their thoughts. 'It's inhuman! They are without pity, Glik and the Fat One. Can we not stop it?'

Someone cursed, 'It's that Glik; he's the one!'

But someone else snarled, 'It's Le Gros. He's there and it's by his orders that this torture's going on. Le Gros is the more responsible for this crime!'

But the torture was over, if they had known it. A prisoner was confessing that he might have let someone climb into that window, perhaps by negligence. Perhaps he had left his post for a short while during the night; he couldn't say so with exactness, but perhaps he did. Just now he couldn't remember, he couldn't swear to anything. Perhaps if they let him alone for a while he would remember. Anything, he would say anything, *only don't let Sergeant Glik loose on him again*. Better kill him out of hand than that.

Le Gros, unmoved, was listening to it all with satisfaction, saying, 'It is as I thought. There has been complicity. We shall find that perhaps there are several in this; perhaps it is a big plot to overthrow authority. Who knows what men will do in their madness.'

And then, just then, they heard the alarm sound from the walls around them.

Perhaps under the circumstances the guards high up on the walls can be excused for some slight negligence that afternoon; for it was only slight. You cannot remain up on an exposed catwalk, with nothing before you but a desert that is always dreary and deserted and not find a sudden and passionate interest in things that shouldn't be of concern to sentries.

During the interrogation of the prisoners most of the wall guards had kept one eye on the punishment cells where their comrades were suffering hell; and that is no way to watch out for stealthy movement far away on the desert plain.

So it was with such surprise that for a second he couldn't believe his eyes, that Legionnaire Alfredo Rappioli glanced aimlessly out on the desert and saw the Arab. Then he opened his lungs and yelled.

Every sentry suddenly gave full attention to his job. Every sentry suddenly saw the same sight. In a gigantic ring around the fortress was a circle of mounted Arabs. Behind were the warriors on foot.

They had come up suddenly from concealment, on a signal, and now were poised, waiting. Pennants were fluttering on the slim-bladed lances; the robes of the cavalry provided a rich and unusual splash of colour against the drab desert. But there was a flash of steel that destroyed any pleasure that the barbaric picture might have contained.

And yet they didn't attack. They just sat their horses and watched from a distance.

L'Irrité heard the shout and came rushing out of the office. Le Gros lurched round the corner from the punishment cells at the same moment. They collided, and L'Irrité nearly fell; as it was his hat rolled into the dust.

Le Gros, he of the insensitive bulk, snapped, 'Fool, get out of my way,' and ran up the steps of the centre block where he could get a clear view round most of the horizon. L'Irrité felt savage. Always things happened to make him feel a fool. The men must be in perpetual laughter at him. All the same he ran up the steps after Le Gros. He might hate the fat officer, but nevertheless it was comforting to have someone to make the decisions and accept responsibility as Le Gros was doing automatically just now.

Le Gros tilted his fat head and looked through his gold-rimmed pince nez. His eyes widened at the sight. Rumour had not exaggerated. Here were thousands of hostile Arabs, and the expected attack appeared momentarily imminent.

Le Gros shouted orders — every man to defence posts; ammunition must be brought out and placed ready to hand. One order after the other. The final one to

L'Irrité, to supervise the distribution of grenades and ammunition. Then he remembered the flag. This was no time to heed such trifles as tribute to the dead. He ordered it to be raised. The tricolour must be on high when the attack came.

But the attack didn't come. That ring of Arabs sat there, unmoving, while inside the fort feverish preparations were made to deal with them. An hour or so later the cavalry retired; then Arab tents sprang up, and the fortress knew that this was to be a siege.

Le Gros thumped down into the guardroom. The thought of battle made him feel quite cheerful. He gave orders for a close watch to be kept on the Arabs, but ordered half the men to return to their rooms.

Zirko of the bad teeth, that Swiss sergeant so unlike Willi Pretel, the Swiss legionnaire, was on duty now. He chased the men and got them away to rest or duties, as the case might be, then returned to his commanding officer.

Le Gros sat on the trestle table within the orderly room and listened to the reports, all momentarily reassuring. He could not understand why an Arab offensive hadn't been mounted, but he was quite content to sit and wait and let the desert brethren camp at his gates. Time was on his side.

Sergeant Zirko was allowed to stand easy in his presence, and even invited to discuss the reports as they came in. Big, steel-toothed Glik was up at the wall controlling the defence for the moment. None could be better in a fight than the Latvian.

In good humour, Le Gros was pleased to speak his thoughts aloud. This fortress was strong, almost impregnable; a frontal attack such as had seemed imminent would certainly have been repulsed with heavy losses to the attacking force. Therefore they had changed their minds and gone over to a war of patience; they would starve the garrison out, these Arabs thought in their ignorance.

L'Irrité came in on the last few sentences. Le Gros's complacency affected his nerves like the sound of a drill to a man in a dentist's chair. He said, 'You are so sure, Anton; always you are so sure. But, *mon dieu*, after seeing all those Arabs out there I am sure of nothing.' He spread his soft white hands and his brown eyes held fears and forebodings, worries and uncertainties. 'You must admit, Anton, never have we seen so many war-like Arabs in arms against us before. Why, then, do you treat it all like a joke? You are almost laughing.' He was irritated by that good humour, when he felt nothing but anxiety.

Le Gros had to go through those motions of adjusting his glasses before gazing at the nervous, smaller officer and saying, so heavily that it could have been contempt only it was just a way of speaking — 'They can sit out there as long as they like. The longer the better. Soon help will come to us, and then we shall sally out of this fort and — ' he cracked the haunches of two heavy hands together suddenly — 'then we will break them like a nut within its cracker.'

Emile Zirko was taking no part in this conversation, but his eyes were contemptuous as he watched the fear that kept rising into the soft pink face of L'Irrité, he who should have taken a cowl and not a kepi. Zirko had no time for cowardice in any man; to him a thing weak was a thing to be crushed . . .

With rising irritation, L'Irrité demanded, 'But how will help come? How will they know that we need it? Le Caporal Brissel failed to get through, and his companions will be sport for the Arab women now.' The thought made him sick.

Le Gros looked over his head, out through the door into the brilliant sunshine; watched the men crouching up there on the catwalks, the blue of their uniforms standing out against the grey wall of the battlemented fortress — over all a sky that was lighter blue, but so intense it gave men an ache at the back of the eyes to stare up at it.

L'Irrité heard the big man say, 'Never you mind, Armaund. It might be a day or two in reaching us — perhaps longer — but assuredly help will come from Alfia.' Then he turned his face towards him and there was something like humour at the back of those spectacles.

And L'Irrité had a feeling that there was something he should have remembered; that what Le Gros was saying should have been as apparent to himself. It made him even more irritable.

He went out and persecuted a few men for the most irritating trifles. One was the unfortunate Albert Volin, who was on guard now, and drooping because he felt sick from the blow on his head. L'Irrité told him to pull himself together; that wasn't the way to look in the face of the enemy.

Which was good, coming from L'Irrité.

In the orderly room Le Gros remembered his decision to move into the late Captain Paon's quarters. He informed Sergeant Zirko of his intentions and gave suitable instructions in regard to his belongings, with especial injunctions regarding the portage of his liquor supplies.

Zirko accepted the order, then, about to go, said. 'What do you think of this theory, *mon lieutenant* — that the assassin of Captain Paon was an Arab?'

6

Bring the flag down

For the moment Le Gros was startled. He was not to know that he was hearing his own words come back to him. He said, 'This is remarkable! What is this theory?'

Zirko shrugged. 'It is among the men. There are some who say that it is an Arab way to treat a man so, and they swear that the assassin came from outside and is not here within the fort.'

Le Gros said again that this was remarkable, and this time he cleaned the steam off his spectacles and regarded the sergeant with thought before replying further. He was trying to fit in this theory with his own momentary views on the subject, that morning up in the tower. Then he shrugged; he had more decisive views in the situation now.

Instead he asked, 'What is your opinion, sergeant?' Because Zirko, for all his malignity towards men, his malice and slyness, had intelligence and was a proven fighter in desert warfare.

Zirko said quite boldly, 'I do not know anything about the killing, *mon lieutenant*. But I have other views on the Arabs out there.' He jerked his head towards the wall.

Le Gros said, 'Oh, yes? Such as, *mon sergent*?'

So Zirko told him. With due diffidence he was not happy about the lieutenant's theory that the Arabs had been about to charge upon the fort only at the last minute to change their mind. He had no real opposition theory, but it seemed stupid tactics, and the leaders of these Arabs were rarely stupid men.

He thought that they had deliberately shown themselves, perhaps with the idea of upsetting the morale of the garrison. They were clever, these Arabs, and that was typical Arab tactics — a war on nerves.

All too well these Arabs knew the strain that a stay at a desert station imposed upon a man; perhaps they felt that if their silent, menacing presence were known it could seriously affect the men. Did the lieutenant not remember the celebrated case of the desert station down at Wadi el Jafna? There a silent watching Arab army had so played upon the nerves of the garrison that some of the men under a foolish lieutenant had gone out to precipitate action. He and his men had not come back, and the fortress had nearly fallen in consequence of the lack of these men.

Le Gros said, 'That will not happen here. So how does that affect your theory, *mon sergent*? What do you think they will do in that event?'

That Zirko did not know. But if he had cast his mind back to the previous morning, when the dust devils were about, he might have had a clue.

He was about to depart, but in the doorway he hesitated. '*Mon lieutenant*,' he murmured, 'there might be something in what the men say.'

'That Captain Paon's murderer was an Arab?'

'Just that. Could it be that it is part of

an Arab war on our nerves?'

Le Gros began to laugh. His laugh grew louder. Then the scorn poured into it. 'Oh, *mon ami*, you are beginning to frighten yourself, I can see. But it will not frighten me. Tonight I sleep in Captain Paon's room. And why?'

He pushed his face close to the sergeant's, then hurriedly withdrew it. Zirko's breath was as bad as his teeth.

'Why, because I shall know the assassin in a matter of hours. Send Glik to me.'

But he didn't know, not that afternoon. Because a man can stand just so much and then he seeks protection in unconsciousness. And the men's cries did more to harm the morale of the legionnaires than all the Arabs camped outside.

★   ★   ★

There is always something unreal about awakening in the desert. The light is too bright; there is too much of sky and sand; and colours seem always too colourful to be true. For the first minutes after waking, men have to adjust themselves to this unreal world that has been decanted on them on the heels of sleep.

So it was that when Willi Pretel and the bony, scrub-haired Englishman, Peter Warr, came slowly across to the ablutions they had that distant sense of unreality of an early desert awakening.

So it was that when they saw an officer's servant shouting through a keyhole, up the steps of the tower, they had that feeling, 'I have seen all this before.'

Zirko came running across, aroused by the noise, with big Glik, steel teeth gleaming against the lather on his chin. They pounded up the stone steps, Zirko shouting, 'What is it? Why do you shout so?' Though he thought he knew, even so quickly.

The legionnaire was frightened and turned wide eyes towards them. '*Le lieutenant*, he does not answer.'

Glik shoved him on one side, roughly, because how else can a man be shoved aside by a sergeant of the legion? He stooped and bellowed through the repaired lock keyhole, then rattled the iron ring of a handle as if he would drag it off.

And Le Gros made no answer.

They were coming out now, half-dressed men brought from their morning preparations by the swift flash of news that something was wrong. High up on the walls, the sentries started to get interested, also, but then Big Glik, the Latvian, turned suddenly and bellowed at them, and after that they faced out to the desert. There was, after all, an enemy outside.

Glik kicked the door a few times, though he knew it would produce no result. Then he turned and ordered, 'You and you, get axes and bars.' And again it was Willi Pretel who happened to be in the forefront of the spectators, so that again it was Willi the Swiss who swung that axe mightily and shattered — this time beyond repair — that long-suffering lock.

The long bolt offered stouter resistance, but the heel of the axe in time drove that off its seating and then the door swung open.

The Englishman was the other man

with Pretel. He had watched his companion, his mouth slightly open, showing that childish omission of front teeth; his eyes that never showed weariness, anger, hate, frustration or other human emotions, carried only their look of absorbed interest in the proceedings.

When Pretel paused, the bolt nearly away, the big, bony Englishman stepped forward, pushed hard and fell into the tiny passage.

When he arose he saw Le Gros looking at him. Le Gros with a curved Arab sword by his side and his head held to his body only by the tough, resistant bone of his spine.

Sergeant Glik roared, 'Go, summon *le lieutenant*,' and under his breath cursed the weakling for having to be sent for. He should have been here; a good officer should have been attracted by the commotion long ago, instead of lying abed. And he found himself thinking that with the enemy at their gates they would need a good officer now, whereas they only had — L'Irrité!

The thought sent him suddenly racing

across and up to the wall post, so that he could look out for himself and estimate any possible threat from the enemy. Legionnaire Warr saw him go and understood, and Willi Pretel heard him say something softly in Arabic.

Willi Pretel, standing hushed in the presence of tragedy, murmured, 'You said, *mon ami*?'

Warr shrugged, disclaiming. 'It is nothing; it is a quotation from a celebrated writer. It means, 'It was in the time of the season of the winds'.'

Pretel looked into those wide, innocent eyes and said, 'I do not understand.'

Warr gazed after the sergeant, high up on the wall now, but said nothing further. Instead he turned and looked at the sack-like body of their late commander, his Paris silk pyjamas tied across the fat stomach that would never again clamour for earthly pleasures. Pretel found himself watching the reaction of the legionnaire. It was so unnatural, that a man could look upon grotesque and terrible death like that and not show any emotion other than mild interest.

And yet that was all that he could see in those childish blue eyes.

Warr said, 'It was a touch of humour, of the macabre, yes, to fix his glasses to that pudding of a nose.' And Willi, so well brought up by quiet, God-fearing parents back in Switzerland, was shocked by the remark, though at the back of his staid mind was the thought that there was something comical in those ridiculous glasses, in death resting in their accustomed place.

Glik came across the parade ground again, satisfied, and he met L'Irrité at the foot of the steps. L'Irrité knew there was something very seriously wrong, but he hadn't had the courage to ask the legionnaire who had fetched him. But sometime he had to know, so he said to Sergeant Glik, 'There is something wrong, yes?'

Glik the Latvian answered heavily, 'Assuredly there is something wrong, *mon commander*.'

L'Irrité stood transfixed, trying to understand the meaning of that last word. Then he did fiddly things with his hands and said, 'I do not understand yet, *sergent*. Please be so good as to tell me . . .'

Glik's steel-toothed mouth opened and he told him brutally. 'The commander is dead — killed . . . murdered in his sleep like Captain Paon. Now you are the commander, *mon lieutenant*.'

He watched closely as he spoke, and he saw all that was in the officer's soul, because the shock of the announcement stripped him bare of pretence. L'Irrité was horrified. And it wasn't horror at the thought of the death of Le Gros . . . it was personal, a dismay beyond expression at the thought that he, L'Irrité, was now in charge of this fortress, with all that that implied.

He panicked, and an officer should never panic in the presence of a subordinate. He said the worst thing he could have said in the presence of the harsh, unfeeling Glik, though true it was a whisper and wasn't perhaps intended for those misshapen ears. He said, '*Mon dieu*, what am I to do?'

And Glik showed the beginning of what

was to come. He rasped, 'You will be fort commander, *mon lieutenant*,' and it is doubtful if he could have got away with such a tone if it had been addressed to either of the preceding commanders. But then he would certainly never have used such an expression of speech to them.

L'Irrité never noticed it. He looked unhappily up the steps. A couple of legionnaires and Sergeant Emile Zirko stood at attention at the top, waiting for him to ascend. He thought how colourful they looked, with their red trousers and the low-slanting sun gilding their faces, and high above them the clear colours of the lazy-floating tricolour of France set against the brilliance of the blue African sky.

Then he looked at Glik and he knew that he had to do something, knew he had to say something. So he said, irritably, 'Why do you speak to me with your face covered in soap, Sergeant Glik? Go clean yourself, immediately.'

It did a lot of harm, that outburst of petty irritation. Glik saluted, said nothing, but turned and went back to his quarters. But he was thinking, and now malice tinged his thoughts.

Now alone, L'Irrité slowly mounted the steps, trying to consider what should be done. He didn't want to look at his dead comrade, but there was nothing else for it now — he was fort commander, and this was part of his new duties.

As he went in out of the sunshine that was already too hot for comfort, his face blanched, meeting those eyes behind those absurd gold-rimmed pince-nez. Blood always upset him; this overwhelmed him and he had to look quickly away or else he would have been sick.

He thought, frantically, 'What should I do? What is expected of me?' And then, fortunately, he remembered the pattern that had been set by his predecessor, now in turn the corpse.

Now, what had Le Gros done under similar circumstances? He thought for a moment. Why, yes, he had looked round to see what could be seen. So he would look round and see what could be seen. Anyway, that would keep his eyes away from the horrible bulk that had been Le Gros.

With a pang he remembered his thoughts of yesterday, that viciousness that had prompted him to wish that Le Gros might lose his fat head. Well, it had happened, and, dear God, how he wished it hadn't! At that moment he would have given anything to have had Le Gros alive and fort commander again — anything rather than that he should have to make decisions and fight a war against an army of Arabs . . . Gladly now would he have suffered the coarseness and gross offensiveness of the big man's conduct, if only he could be alive and with him.

He found himself moaning, and quickly stopped himself, because that curious English legionnaire had those strange wide-open eyes watching him interestedly. A strange man, this Britisher, and he disturbed him always. There was something about him that was not of other men . . .

He thought, 'Look around, as Anton did, and see what there is to see.'

But there was nothing to see, or very

little. The disordered bed, with the bloodstains that indicated a death stab during sleep; the table with its crowd of bottles and a decanter that wasn't used because Le Gros never had time to fill a decanter only to empty it again into his stomach.

Ah, there was that open window. He went to it, as Anton had done, and looked down on the wall, and on the sentry with his rifle pointing out through an embrasure towards an enemy unseen from this angle. And beyond was the great expanse of desert, and the blue hills in the lazy distance that rose low and rounded into the harder blue of the sharp morning sky.

The window was wide open, as wide as it could be — as wide as it would have to be if a man were to leave or enter by it.

L'Irrité could make nothing of it, and now he walked quickly to the door, anxious to get out from this atmosphere of death. But Zirko stopped him, almost barred his way. His bad teeth showed and in that shaded light his eyes seemed to gleam unnaturally bright. The lieutenant thought how curious it was that this morning he should be able to notice such details when he never remembered seeing them with such clarity before. This tragedy seemed to have sharpened his mind for the trivial and the unimportant, to the exclusion of what he should have seen . . .

Sergeant Zirko said, 'Mon *lieutenant*, there is this sword that you have not examined.'

L'Irrité looked at it. There was blood on it. 'Yes, yes,' he said. 'It was that that killed poor Armaund.' And he felt a hypocrite for using the adjective poor.

Emile Zirko persisted. 'But yes, *mon lieutenant*. But is there not something to be remarked about the sword. As, for instance, that it is of Arab workmanship?'

Now, L'Irrité knew there was significance in that remark, and knew that he should react suitably, but for the life in him he was so stupid that it passed over his head and he could only stare at the sergeant.

So the sergeant said, 'Do you not remember . . . that theory among the men? That perhaps the assassin of

Captain Paon was an Arab?'

L'Irrité understood. He forced himself to look at that curving broad blade with its ornate handle, though the near-black of the bloodstains revolted his stomach. Yes, undoubtedly that was an Arab sword.

He said, 'There are many such within the barracks — souvenirs that men have collected from time to time.' But he did not feel convinced.

Zirko had walked to the window and was looking out, and as helpless as the old woman that he felt himself to be, the lieutenant followed.

Zirko said, 'I do not see how it can be. Though it would be easy to place a plank from the top of the wall and rest it on the sill and then walk in.' He considered. 'But there is the matter of getting up the wall. Perhaps the assassin could have used a scaling pole.' That was a pole with pegs stuck alternately so as to form a ladder.

He turned quickly, and the evil that was in his bad stomach fanned into the lieutenant's face and made him recoil in disgust.

'But yes, do you not see? He could

climb the wall with the pole, then use it to bridge this gap while he came inside and slaughtered *les officiers*. That would be nothing to these Arabs, for they are as cats and could walk comfortably upon a piano wire if they chose.'

L'Irrité looked out and saw the boarded catwalk and thought what a fascinating pattern the wall defences made from this angle. He dragged back his thoughts and said, 'There is the matter of the sentry, immediately below this window. Have you forgotten him, *mon sergent*? Consider. Could anyone creep up from the desert undetected, and, still without detection, climb first the outer wall, and then across this gap here into this room? It would be an incredible performance, would it not?'

The sergeant threw out both his hands in a gesture of helplessness. '*Mon lieutenant*, that is only how it can be, unless this is the work of the devil.'

L'Irrité moved back from the window. He was suddenly thinking, 'Thank God the pattern is not quite the same. Thank God there is no severed head and limb as in the case of Captain Paon and the legionnaire Planche.' That would have been too much for him, he knew it would. Even this was too bad.

Carefully avoiding that silly corpse with its ludicrous pince-nez on the bloodless fleshy nose, he wondered at the difference. Then he shrugged. Of course there could be many reasons. The assassin might have been disturbed; or simply he might not have intended a repetition of previous atrocities. After all, thought L'Irrité, even an assassin must find a certain monotony in following too closely to a pattern. It could have been too much for him after repeating on Paon what he had done to Legionnaire Planche . . .

L'Irrité pulled himself up with a jerk. What was he thinking? If he ascribed to the murderer of Paon the death of Planche, then it could only mean that he also considered the assassin was an Arab — or Arabs, of course.

He said aloud, 'But that is fantastic.'

And he of the bad teeth said, 'But of course it cannot be the work of the devil. I was not serious, *mon lieutenant*.' For

L'Irrité's words had come after the sergeant's previous comment, and he thought that the officer's expostulation was in reference to that.

L'Irrité looked vaguely at him, not understanding. And then again he spoke aloud, and again showed his weakness. For he said, 'What is there now that we can do?'

Zirko slowly drooped his eyelids, so that the contempt would not show. After deliberation he said carefully, 'I would question the sentries who were on guard under this window last night, just as the lieutenant' — he jerked a hand to indicate the silent hulk on the floor — 'just as he did.'

'You mean, in the punishment cells?' L'Irrité's blood chilled at the thought of having to stand witness to such 'questioning'.

'*Dans les cellules,*' agreed Zirko with emphasis. 'Who knows, perhaps they are complicit in the crime, just as the lieutenant considered. I would get the truth from them, if there is any truth in these wretches.'

Wearily the new fort commander pointed

out an obvious thing. 'The lieutenant' — indicating the corpse — 'considered he had obtained the truth from those wretches yesterday, that they were complicit in some plot against Captain Paon. All night they have been prisoners in the cells, yet death has reached out for the man who placed them there. Your theory is interesting, sergeant, but futile.'

He looked at the Arab sword, shuddered delicately and turned away. 'Oil and water do not mix, Sergeant Zirko. You cannot entertain a theory which embraces an Arab assassin with legionnaire conspirators.' L'Irrité had an involved personality, but he was not unintelligent.

Zirko's face fell. Perhaps he had looked forward to taking Glik's place in a bout of 'questioning'. They passed out together, so that they stood in the doorway with a view that commanded most of the desert.

Then L'Irrité remembered something that Le Gros had done yesterday, and gladly he was able to give an order. 'Have the flag lowered to half-mast, Sergeant Zirko.'

Zirko hesitated, then transmitted the

order to Legionnaire Pretel. Pretel unfastened the cords and slowly the flag came down. L'Irrité remembered what Le Gros had done at that, and brought himself up to the salute.

Then he felt foolish, realising why Zirko had hesitated. There were Arabs camped at their gates, and that was no time to lower the flag. Quickly he turned, to hide his discomfiture, but he hadn't the courage to reverse his order. He saw the men crowding at the foot of the steps, and it gave him an opportunity to work off his momentary embarrassment. He shouted, 'Get those men back to their duties, sergeant. Must they stand about like sheep when there is much to do?'

Then he went back to his quarters and felt ill. He was trembling, looking at his white face in the mirror; horrified to think that the safety of this fort and all within it depended upon his courage and resource. For he knew he was a man without courage and without the slightest evidence of resource in all his career.

'I must pull myself together,' he thought, but he was panic-stricken. If only he could emulate the massive calm of Anton; if only he had the same sureness in himself! But he hadn't. And then he found himself thinking, 'If only I could find the repose and solace in strong drink, as Anton seemed to do,' and because there was an idea in it and something to do he gave an order for the late lieutenant's liquor to be brought to him, he not having the courage to face that scene again.

He was no drinking man, with the result that in a very little time he was considerably drunk. But drink affects men differently. In the new fort commander's case, it merely exaggerated where he had hoped to subdue; where he had been emotional before, he was hysterical now — he had been terrified but had tried not to show it; but now it was there, leaping out of his eyes, showing in the twitching white face, and betraying him at every word with his tongue.

But even before this, Zirko went across and sat down with Glik. And then they spoke of things that are unusual in the minds of soldiers of the Legion.

7

The madness of Legionnaire Dalarge

Willi Pretel, the Swiss, stood courteously aside at the barrack room door for his companion to enter ahead of him. Equally courteous, the gap-toothed, scrub-haired Englishman insisted politely, 'No, my friend, after you.'

They passed in from the blinding sunshine, then stood as they always stood, so that their eyes could get accustomed to the comparative gloom of the long, low-ceilinged — too low for comfort — room. It was whitewashed, very clean, and the windows were open so as to let in any breeze, but only waves of heat crept in from the baking parade ground and with it a fine powder of dust. However, the roof hid away the pitiless glaring sun, and that was something.

As they stood together the tall Englishman said, 'It is the season of the winds,' and he was looking through a window at a distant patch of blue across which trailed a wisp of swift-moving cloud.

Willi Pretel remembered that that was what he had said in Arabic, an hour or so ago. He said, 'You speak Arabic, *mon ami?*'

'Tolerably.' The Englishman nodded. He was watching a group of men around Fiertel's bed, and that expression of intense interest showed in his curious blue eyes . . . curious because of that light that seemed to put him apart from other men.

'But where did you learn it?' There had been little time since the Englishman joined them for him to have studied the language overmuch; for most of it had been spent in towns and posts surrounded by hostile natives.

Those blue eyes came round and fixed themselves with interest on Pretel's broad-cheeked, healthy-red face.

'In the Sudan, in Egypt.' He shrugged his craggy shoulders. 'In other places. I was in the British campaigns against the Mad Mahdi. Kitchener was our general. I learned a lot about the Arabs.'

He was looking back at Fiertel's party; Chopin, the unconscious propagandist, was talking — talking with his mouth, with his, big rolling eyes, with his hands — aye, with his arms right beyond his elbows. Chopin was believing in his own propaganda, and was desperate now to convince others.

Pretel started to move across to his bed, drooping from the short fatigue in the heat of that early morning. He said something in his tiredness, not the kind of thing good Willi Pretel normally said; but sometimes there comes to all of us a moment when words edge their way from our mouths and we regret them immediately afterwards.

He said, 'You must have learned a lot about treachery, then.' But then Willi Pretel was, after all, a legionnaire, and that was the way a legionnaire was taught to regard their traditional enemies.

He was astounded. The big Englishman turned and took him earnestly by the shoulder and said, 'You are wrong, Willi. The history of the Arab people is that the treachery has been mostly against them — from their own leaders as well as from we infidels. Can you wonder, with the awful oppression imposed by European powers, that they sometimes react violently? Wouldn't you, Willi? Wouldn't I?'

It was startling; these were sentiments never uttered in a Legion barrack room. Willi could only look into those intent earnest blue eyes.

'You see,' said the curious Englishman (weren't all Englishmen supposed to be mad? Willi suddenly thought), 'You see, they are made to suffer so, these poor people. Nature is against them, and so apparently is every other wealthy nation; they are ground down, and are treated as a slave people. We — we, the Foreign Legion — are the instruments of the oppression — '

Good-hearted Willi was distressed. He grabbed the legionnaire by the arm and looked quickly round. Francois Delpage was within earshot, and he was a notorious tattler to authority.

'*Mon enfant*,' he exclaimed, 'what are you saying? If this were known higher up you would be sent to the penal battalions.'

And the Englishman. What did he say to that? That look of interest came back into his eyes and he said, 'You know, I've heard so much about those places. I wonder if they are as bad as they are made out to be? I would like to know . . . ' Then he seized Willi again, and be was smiling. 'But you wouldn't tell, *mon ami*, I know.' And then he patted the big Swiss and went to his bed and began the eternal, never-ending task of cleaning kit and equipment.

Pretel's bed was close to Fiertel's — too close. So that Chopin's harangue was audible to him — too audible.

And Chopin was on again about his theory of yesterday. They had laughed at him, he declared indignantly, when he said that the commander's assassin was an Arab. But were they laughing today? Oh, no, they were laughing on the other side of their faces; and he gave what he considered an imitation of people performing that, after all, impossible act.

For was it not obvious now even to

their dull heads that the assassin of both their late commanders was an Arab?

He waited for an answer, but none came. So he went on. Now, to the little Chopin it was a kind of battle — he was the kind of man who must not only share his beliefs around but must also insist that others accept the beliefs as implicitly as he did himself. Such men can be a nuisance in a small community such as a barrack room contained; and sometimes they can be dangerous.

Le Gros who was a pig, and weren't pigs notoriously stupid, had been sure that one or the other of the sentries had killed Captain Paon. True, it was just possible that a man in such a position so high up on a catwalk could have climbed across a plank or ladder and gained access through that unlocked window. But what man in his right senses would perform such a crime, knowing that suspicion must fall upon him immediately after the event? And neither of those men was *cafard*, were they? he demanded belligerently.

For some reason Fiertel was now

finding all this very interesting. But then he had the dull, brutish mind that requires the sensational to make any impact at all upon his consciousness. And the close-cropped, scar-headed Tissdan was sucking a hollow tooth and finding it absorbing, also; so Schweld and Le Groneau, Dalarge, Puty, Hassvas and the others had decided to give Chopin a hearing, too.

Such an audience makes a man bold, and boldness adds conviction to any argument.

Now Chopin spread his hands and said, 'Mes enfants, in any event was not Le Gros proved wrong by the very circumstances of his death? Could either of those men have been the assassin of Captain Paon, and Lieutenant Le Gros? Why, how could they, when Le Gros had them locked up all night?'

The assassin was an Arab, he insisted, or possibly more than one Arab, and the whole thing was part of an Arab plot to deprive the garrison of their leaders at a time when they needed them most. That was why they were waiting at the gates

— *waiting until one by one the Rosí had lost all its leaders.*

It was a sensational theory, the sort of idea that comes to a fevered little imagination like Chopin's — an inspiration that suddenly had the barrack room on its feet.

Because it seemed the only credible explanation for a wholly incredible affair.

The men were talking, excited; and the excitement of one fed the excitement of another, as is the way in crowds, so that within seconds the room was a-roar with men's shouting voices.

It was so, they were saying; it could be. These Arabs was it not notorious that they could come and go without being seen at any time? And then they started to remind each other of the old soldiers' tales, of Arabs who had crept into barrack rooms and removed the breech mechanism of rifles that were lying at their sleeping owners' sides. In a moment it was completely accepted that in some way the besieging Arabs had found a secret method of entering and leaving the fortress.

Then a note that was akin to panic and even hysteria crept into the shouting. It was like wine to the arguing, gesticulating, shouting little sneak thief named Chopin. It was fuel that fed the fires of his inspiration, and turned his fevered brain ever the faster.

'You see,' he shouted recklessly. 'They will come again. Again you will see them strike. L'Irrité is next to go, mark my words. And then — then it will be the turn of the Trinity, and we shall be left to defend this post without leaders!'

For just one moment that was too much to be accepted. For a second the wild prophecy was greeted with an outburst of humour. 'Hurrah for the killer,' someone called. 'The sooner we are without Glik and that foul Zirko the better!'

And another voice shouted, 'Glik deserves to die for what he did to those men yesterday,' and this time it was the voice of Sebastian Dalarge. Pretel looked up in dismay. It was bad when this folly spread to good, quiet men; for though Dalarge was a solitary man, he was yet

118

regarded as a good, steady soldier.

The cry was taken up, and in the savagery of the moment that flash of humour died, never to be reborn. The damage was done.

Glik was a fiend, they murmured, and it was like a sullen wave washing round the room, low and growling and threatening. For what he had done to their comrades, nothing was too bad for him, they said, and now it was no longer a murmur but a roar that rose and filled the room. Glik deserved to die, they shouted; he was not fit to live; he was a spawn of hell and the devil couldn't claim him fast enough!

Pretel rose quickly and began to cross to Dalarge, he of the bandaged hands. For the legionnaire was standing, his face curiously white, his eyes fixed and burning, and he was repeating what was being said.

Pretel put his hand on his shoulder and shouted, 'You are not well, my son. You must not mix with these foolish people. Come and sit with me.' And like the father he was to many a young legionnaire, the big Swiss took him out of the barrack room.

Glik came doubling across the parade ground towards the scene of the commotion.

Pretel felt the shoulder begin to tremble under his hand at sight of the big sergeant. 'Be quiet,' he whispered urgently. 'There is going to be trouble now; you don't want any of it, Sebastian, do you?'

But Dalarge spoke as if Pretel's words had never been uttered. 'They are right; Glik is unfit to live. If there were any justice in the world he would have died long ago for the evil in his heart. It is a sign that there is no God.'

Good Willi Pretel was shocked. He said, 'Hush, *mon ami*, that is no way to talk.'

Glik was almost up to them now, his steel teeth bared and glinting in his savage face. The commotion still went on behind them.

Pretel felt his arm caught. 'I beg you to restrain me, my good friend, or I will kill him now,' he heard the man say. He was ill, ill in his mind; Willi should have noticed it before.

'Justice,' Dalarge was whispering as

Glik stamped past them. 'Justice is what the world is crying for. It is the duty of men always to see that justice is done.' He was still holding on to the unhappy Swiss legionnaire's sleeve, his burning brown eyes seeming to try to probe into Willi Pretel's skull.

'Oh, Willi Pretel, I know what I'm talking about. My people had religion; in its name they did terrible things to me. They said I was born in sin and I was unclean and a reproach to them in the eyes of the Lord.

'So many times a week I was consigned into the darkness of a cellar so that I could pay penance for what I had done by being born to them. M'sieur, I was but a child, a very small child. And, m'sieur, my father was a tanner, and that cellar was under the warehouse, and, m'sieur, have you ever seen the size of rats that feed on the leather in a tannery?'

His eyes were growing bigger, going into the past in his memory. 'I can see them now, so big, and their eyes shining hungrily at me. And I was such a little child, and I had never done anything wrong, I'd never done . . . '

His voice was screaming. Willi put his hand across his mouth and stopped him. He was distressed by the smaller man's suffering, and he, a religious man, bowed his head in agony to think of the evils that are perpetrated in the name of God.

Odd Skadshaim slipped out around Glik and came and put a restraining hand on the struggling legionnaire. '*Cafard*,' whispered Willi, but he said it bitterly. Poor Sebastian, it seemed not without cause.

Glik was roaring for silence. And he got it. He was standing, straddle-legged just inside that room, his shoulders so broad they kept the sun out . . . his teeth a rat-trap that clashed menacingly at the men.

'Swine!' he called them. '*De quoi s 'agit-il?* Are you all raving mad?'

Suddenly silent, the legionnaires were transfixed at the far end of the room. But as the seconds passed, they thawed a little; they were in dangerous mood, sullen and hostile to the authority that was weakening above them, an authority that they now felt certain would become still weaker. Their heads were lowered, their eyes hard and menacing, and Glik was aware of it.

He kicked a man near him. It was no gentle kick and the man collapsed with a cry and held his thigh in agony. 'You,' stormed Glik, 'tell me what it was all about?' And he poised his foot for another blow.

And the man was Le Groneau, the teller of tales — perhaps it was no accident that he was picked upon by the sergeant.

Le Groneau shouted from the floor, 'It was not my fault, *mon sergent*. It was the Legionnaire Chopin. He is of the opinion that Arabs killed our two commanders, and he is of the opinion that you will shortly die, too.'

Now, Le Groneau need not have said so much, but he was in agony from that blow, and he wanted others to share the suffering, forgetting that pain is not something that can be shared.

Chopin went white. Schweld stirred uneasily and whispered, '*Son affaire est faite*.' Most definitely Chopin was in for it!

Glik the Latvian shouted in fury, 'What is that I hear? Is that wretch threatening my life?' An interpretation that no reasonable man would have taken from the context of Le Groneau's speech, but then Glik did not owe his position to his capacity for reasoning.

'Come here!' he bellowed. 'You will come with me for interrogation in the office. Perhaps you know more about these affairs than we think.'

Le Groneau was balanced on one leg now as the white-faced Chopin came reluctantly along the room. Chopin kicked him viciously, suddenly, and Le Groneau fell howling against the sergeant. Glik lifted a big hand and cut down savagely behind Le Groneau's ear. The legionnaire stopped howling and slumped on to his face, whimpering quietly.

Glik kicked Chopin out ahead of him. He felt pleased. There were people in Paris who were saying that N.C.O.s of the Foreign Legion should not strike men. It was nonsense, of course, but nowadays one had to exercise a little care in the execution of one's duties. He shrugged, perplexed. After all, what was there to being an N.C.O. if one was to be deprived of the pleasure that kicking a man around gave? None, absolutely none.

The sun in their faces, Willi Pretel, Dalarge and the Norwegian watched the unhappy little Chopin march briskly across to the orderly room. Then Dalarge, not trembling any longer, said, as if he had not been interrupted:

'They were so big, those rats, they would in time have killed me. Sometimes I had to fight them off with my little feet, yet my parents hardened their ears to my infant screams of terror. Oh, God, what I suffered! Oh, God, what I am still suffering now as a result of it!'

Willi said: 'Don't think of it, my child. Why torture yourself with memories? Forget it, and make the most of your life here in the Legion.'

'Forget it?' Dalarge's head came round slowly, so that those eyes were burning into Pretel's skull again. 'Can I ever forget my torment when hourly the injustice all about me is a constant reminder of those terrible days?'

He walked slowly into the shade of the now subdued barrack room. Just inside, he half turned and said: 'But I found a way of getting out of reach of those rats. Some day I will tell you about it.'

8

Their Commander Was Drunk

Again it was le Legionnaire Putôt, the Paralysed One, who roused the garrison with a warning cry half an hour later. He was at a post on the south wall, just beyond the long low barrack room.

In that time much had happened. Sergeant Glik had taken it upon himself to order the tricolour to be raised on high again. It was significant that he did so without first seeking the approval of the commanding officer; but the new commander was in a noisy state of drunkenness, and was an active incitement to undisciplined conduct.

Not that Glik the Latvian considered it in any way an act of indiscipline. To him, a crude-thinking soldier, it was wrong that with the enemy at the gate, the flag should be anywhere but at the masthead; and if the commander was too drunk to

127

realise it, why, he, Sergeant Wilhelm Glik, next in order of rank, would see that it was put there. And he did.

Yet Sergeant Wilhelm Glik the Latvian would never have presumed to such an act if Le Gros had been the commanding officer and drunk into the bargain. Drunk or not, Le Gros was a man, a gentleman, and an officer of France. L'Irrité, he of the twitching white and worried eyes, was none of these.

So it was that with this simple act of insubordination the big sergeant did, in effect, take control over the defences of the fortress.

L'Irrité had forgotten to give orders about the disposal of the late lieutenant, who was known for good reason generally as *Le Gros*. Glik of the steel mouth had him boxed up, then ceremoniously buried him in a corner of the fort . . . It would have been inviting trouble to have had him taken and buried outside alongside Captain Paon.

Then he ordered a machine-gun — this weapon new, in those days, to the Foreign Legion — to be posted atop of the tower, and that caused trouble.

There had always been private debate on the value of a gun up there. Captain Paon always had one mounted on this, the highest point, in time of attack; Le Gros had been of the opinion that it was a waste of a good weapon, because it could only cover that part of the desert well beyond the fortress walls. Far better to have it over, say, the main gate, was his argument.

From a military point of view, Le Gros was undoubtedly correct, and the old-fashioned Paon had been in considerable error. But Glik the Latvian, a soldier for years under Paon, understood not the subtleties of the matter and because Captain Paon had a liking for a machine gun up in that apparently commanding position, why, he too decided it must be better there. And in the end it turned out well that he followed the captain's theory . . .

Sergeant Etienne Phare saw the machine gun being hoisted up the steel ladder, and he knew that their new, if drunk, commanding officer had not ordered it to be taken up there. For one thing, because he was too drunk to give such an order; another, because L'Irrité, who was intelligent if a poor soldier, had agreed with Le Gros that the tower was a poor place for the siting of their one machine gun.

Sergeant Phare rushed up in a passion at once. Who had given this order? On what authority were they taking the machine gun up those steps?

The two men clung to the ladder, the machine gun a heavy link between them. They were anxious, because Phare could be a devil when he went into one of his tempers. They looked down and said quickly they had orders from Sergeant Glik.

For a moment it seemed as though Phare would order them down with the gun, but after a second's gnashing of his toothless mouth, he suddenly charged off down the steps and ran in search of the senior sergeant.

The legionnaires on the wall outside the company office heard the row that ensued. Phare's voice took on that high and strident note that always developed when he was going to bring God in to support his views.

They heard him shout that Glik was guilty of wilful acts of disobedience; that was by his conduct being insubordinate to his commanding officer. Never mind if he was drunk; that wasn't the question. The lieutenant was their superior officer, and it was God's will that men should faithfully serve those appointed to positions over them. And much more about God and the divine right of those appointed to give commands.

He was no hypocrite, Phare, though few men could follow with understanding his theory on this matter of God's chosen servants, those born to be selected to places in authority over other men. He demanded absolute and undeviating obedience from those beneath him, but he also demanded the same for his superiors, and he gave it wholeheartedly himself.

But both Glik and Zirko, the Swiss with the bad teeth and foul breath, were concerned just now with practical matters and had no time for academic theorising. They were soldiers, and they knew that a fortress without a resolute commander would go under when the Arab attack developed. This was no time for talks of God in connection with the siting of a machine gun.

And so they said to Phare, brutally, tersely. And the shouting went on between them until Glik, with unexpected cunning, roared: 'In any event, am I not your senior and therefore your superior? So do as you are told — shut up!'

It did a lot of harm in the barrack rooms, when they heard of the split among the sergeants. The morale of the men was being assailed hourly — first the loss of two good officers and the manner of their going; then the obvious incompetence of their remaining lieutenant, with a bold and ferocious enemy poised ready for attack outside their walls . . . and now the sergeants had taken to squabbling.

Men began to move into one of the huts to listen to some of the strongly opinionated.

And then it was that The Paralysed One saw the Arabs moving, and his cry went ringing round the fortress so that even L'Irrité heard it. Glik and the other two sergeants immediately raced to their posts, calling out the men as they did so. Legionnaires came pouring from their barrack rooms and went swarming up the walls until a solid line of blue coats was crouched behind the embrasures. Only the gap-toothed legionnaire from England seemed to hurry less than the others. When he came out on to the parade ground, he looked up at the sky. There was no wisp of cloud against the blue now, and he shook his head and almost it seemed as though he were disappointed.

A large force of mounted Arabs was massing half a mile away on the western horizon. They were swirling around, coloured cloaks streaming with the movement, like a gigantic whirlpool; then the slow-rising dust cloud came and obscured them.

Then the spearhead of the attack broke through the cloud and began a steady circling movement of the fortress, first south and then towards the east. They seemed to be closing in when they had gained a point south of the fortress — now the force was revealed as some two thousand well-mounted cavalry, the forefront of the force easily to be seen though those behind were almost completely lost in the desert dust that rose from the ground at their thunderous passage.

When they were southeast of Fortress El Zeeb, and directly in line with the mounting morning sun, suddenly there was a cry and the force fanned out into a wide crescent and leapt into speed. Glik roared an order to be ready. The attack was coming.

The Arabs were down over their horses' necks, guns and swords brandished, and as they came nearer they screamed their wild war cries — 'Allah o'akhbar!'

Allah above all . . .

Men shrieking their hate, terrified horses screaming with fear at the sound — hoofs drumming, dust rising and swirling and enveloping the charging, excited horde. Then their guns crackling off in an irregular fusillade as they came within range.

An order from Glik and a crash of rifle fire from the disciplined legionnaires. A few Arabs somersaulted, more horses crashed and broke their necks. Confusion for the moment, and then the horns of the crescent detached from each other at the centre and two Arab forces went circling round the fortress.

Glik ordered independent fire, and the rifles grew hot as the rounds were pumped up them.

But the Arabs were skirting at a distance, and they were difficult targets to hit, so that not many appeared to suffer hurt.

And then the affair ended as abruptly as it had begun. The prongs of the horns united beyond the fortress, and the Arabs galloped away in a long column back to their lines. Over the desert around the fortress a few horses limped, and a handful of Arabs crawled slowly after their more fortunate comrades. Some others lay still, and both Arabs and the Legion let them lie there untended.

The legionnaires relaxed at their posts, watching the danger recede so quickly.

Most were used to Arab warfare and knew what this meant. What had seemed to be a real attack had developed into a feint, designed to test the strength of the defence.

Zirko grinned his bad teeth up at the Latvian and said: 'They would discover if we have one of those chatter guns that they dread so much, yes?' He jerked his head towards the machine gun which had not opened fire during the engagement because the range had been slightly too great. 'Now they are probably jubilant, assured that we are without. But, yes, *mon cher*, Wilhelm, it was good policy after all to site the gun up there.'

He was given to flattery, this Swiss with the low cunning, and the Latvian, unlike the crazy Sergeant Phare, was susceptible to it.

But at that moment, Glik, the steel-toothed, was looking beyond his good friend Sergeant Emile Zirko and seemed not to hear him.

He was looking on to the parade ground. At a man who was standing there. An officer — the drunken L'Irrité.

Armaund had arrived to take charge of the battle, only when it was over.

He was drunk, and he looked drunk. His attire was rumpled and betrayed his condition; and if that were not sufficient, his face told a fuller story.

He swayed, trying to focus on the big Latvian, high up at a defence post along the wall; his mouth was working loosely, as if he had insufficient control over it — his hair hung in a screen through which his uncertain eyes tried to peer.

Glik, who was a soldier through and through, cursed under his breath. This was no way for an officer to appear, not before men who would shortly have to fight for their lives. It was wrong, wrong; this craven should never have been placed in charge of men — he could only reduce their effectiveness by his conduct and so lessen their chances of survival.

He dropped quickly to the ground, disdaining the ladder, and strode across to the drunken fort commander. He saluted, but his face was hard. Reported: 'The enemy has retired. That was a skirmish to test our strength.' He was abrupt, his manner showing his contempt.

L'Irrité hiccupped, and the sound was heard all along the walls where the men were watching and listening while appearing to do neither. It is a bad thing for an officer to hiccup; there is something comical about a hiccup, and no officer can afford to look comical before soldiers of the calibre of the tough legionnaires.

That hiccup probably meant the end of L'Irrité as a fort commander. It certainly did in the eyes of one man, that man standing before him now.

L'Irrité was a menace to everyone's safety. Something would have to be done about it.

And straight away the officer proved himself to be a menace.

He tried to fix the sergeant with his heavy eyes and said: 'They have gone, but they will come back, yes?'

Glik's steel mouth opened and he snapped: 'They will come back, yes. And there are so many of them, we shall be lucky to survive.'

L'Irrité lifted his poor weak face. 'Isn't

there anything we can do, sergeant?'

Glik chopped out the words. 'Yes, we can fight.'

L'Irrité gave a gesture of despair. 'I didn't mean that. Can we not avoid fighting? If we went out and discussed the matter with the Arab leaders . . . ?'

Glik's face almost registered horror. He was so startled at the idea that he wheeled in consternation and looked up at the crouching legionnaires. And he knew that the damage was done. The legionnaires had heard.

They had heard their weakling officer talk such appalling nonsense. Parley with the Arabs, indeed! It was like trying to hold converse with a raging lion, a lion that had suffered and was intent on nothing more than repaying a hundred-fold the hurt it had sustained.

L'Irrité did not understand that look on his sergeant's face. He was not used to strong drink, and the comparatively small amount that he had taken had inflamed his brain. He began to grow excited.

'See, sergeant, it is better that we make the attempt than that we stay here and submit to slaughter. Prepare a horse for me, and I will go out with an escort of legionnaires to speak with the Arab leaders.'

He was so very, very drunk, poor Lieutenant L'Irrité.

Glik looked up and met the eyes of Sergeant Zirko. At once he knew what he must do. He roared: 'Sergeant Zirko, *le lieutenant* has the fever; you will help me take him to his quarters.'

He saw Phare start to run forward too, his eyes ablaze with suspicion. That steel trap opened again, to shout: 'Sergeant Phare, you will take charge of the defence in my absence. *That is an order!*' That stopped the God-invoking sergeant and kept him out of the way.

L'Irrité was confused. Vaguely he realized that here was disobedience to his orders. But he couldn't think with any speed now, and it was not until Zirko came running up and Glik put his heavy hand on his arm that he realized the position.

If he had struggled to assert his authority, even then he might have kept a control over the forces under him, even at that late hour. For an officer can always order legionnaires to shoot those who oppose him . . .

Now, here it must be said that Glik was a brave man. He knew that his conduct was placing his own life in peril, yet he proceeded as he did because he knew that what he was doing was right. It was not for anything personal that he acted as he did against the fort commander; he did it simply because he knew that the safety of the fortress demanded a strong commander, and L'Irrité was a weakling among weaklings.

And Zirko, he of the bad breath, was little behind him in crude, animal courage. Whatever one's faults, you must be bold and courageous simply to hold a position as sergeant in the Legion.

Glik of the steel mouth took the drunken Armaund by the arm, turned him and walked him back to his quarters

And L'Irrité, in front of all those men, quietly submitted and let him do it.

But then L'Irrité was suddenly overwhelmed with tiredness, the heat of the parade ground stirred up the fumes of the alcohol inside his brain and all he wanted now was to sleep, sleep, sleep. If the Arabs came and captured the fortress, what matter? They would bring a sleep that would only end this nightmare for him.

Glik slowly lowered him on to his bed. For a second the lieutenant seemed to recover a little, seemed almost to be coming awake again. Glik looked at the table with its array of bottles. There was one half-full of raw, fiery Cognac.

Glik picked it up, crossed to the door and locked it, and then came back to the bed.

L'Irrité started to struggle off it, as if suddenly frightened by that act of locking the door against possible intruders. But Glik shoved him flat with his heavy hand and said to his brother sergeant, 'Hold his head, Emile. *Le lieutenant* must go to sleep for a long time. A long, long time.'

Glik suddenly sat astride his superior officer, pinioning the arms with his heavy knees, so that he could not move even if he had wished. Zirko took hold of that small head on its weak neck, and he knew what he had to do. He held his commanding officer by the nose, and in time L'Irrité had to open his mouth so as to breathe.

Glik poured raw alcohol into it.

It took them a long time to get that half-bottle of spirit into the feebly moaning and choking officer, but in the end they succeeded.

And when they had finished, L'Irrité lay still on his bed.

9

The Stirrings of Mutiny

There was another part-drunk bottle of cognac on the table, and that the two sergeants shared between themselves when they were finished with L'Irrité. They drank and looked down with contempt at the white form on the bed. It was the contempt of all men who can take their liquor for the man who cannot.

Zirko swallowed noisily, and said: 'There is a lot of good brandy in the wretch — a calamitous waste. And he is so little used to it it might kill him. I have heard of such things happening before.' But he spoke as though it would matter little to his conscience if such a thing did happen to the unfortunate Armaund.

Glik swilled the brandy round his teeth. 'It matters not, any way,' he said contemptuously. 'If *le lieutenant* survives his anaesthetic, he will have no memory of how be came by it. Probably he was so drunk that he will never remember disgracing himself before the men.'

'And if he does?' Zirko spoke carefully.

Glik considered. There was such a possibility.

After a while he said: 'We will make no decisions, eh, Emile? But things might be better all round if our commander died gallantly during an Arab attack, yes?'

Zirko said 'Yes,' and drank again, and his manner was that of a man who is toasting a parting guest.

★ ★ ★

It was afternoon, and the legionnaire who had fought under Kitchener in the Sudan was at his post high up on the wall. From the punishment cells came the sound of cries and blows and curses; for Sergeant Glik, a glutton for duty, was pursuing his theory that truth can be wrung from men's lips if one but knew how hard to wring.

In the cells, along with the first pair of sentries, were the two who had shared duty on the wall below Le Gros's bedroom window during the previous night. Now they were being 'interrogated' in the hope that they would be able to throw some light on this mystery of the two killings.

Though it stirred some men and left them angry and restless, the cries of the men in the punishment cells did not seem to affect the tall, big-boned legionnaire. For that matter he did not seem to be taking his guard duties seriously either; and when he looked across at the Arab encampment, it was merely with the gaze of a man interested in such people.

For the Legionnaire Warr felt pretty sure that there would be no attack mounted that day.

A slight wind stirred the surface dust and a few clouds spiralled for a few feet into the air, danced for a moment or two, and then subsided slowly back into the sand. Heat waves rose, shimmering from the baking hot, glaring desert, so that the distant horizon dithered in a mad oscillation of distortion, and sometimes the distant hills had the effect of becoming detached from the earth and sailing like islands into the sky.

The heat waves poured oppressively over the high walls, an enemy that no amount of guns could keep out — an enemy often more deadly than the Arabs outside. For heat encourages the fast breeding of insects and the rapid spread of deadly germs. And heat — along with monotony and discomfort — can send men mad.

Joseph Tillfru said so. He came to Willi Pretel, who was resting off after a meal unsuited to such heat, a meal consisting mainly of poor bread and bad potatoes. His long Austrian face, with its long, drooping pair of moustaches, was troubled.

'I come to you, Willi,' he murmured, 'because you have the good mind, whereas all men in El Zeeb seem to be going mad.'

His French was bad, and Willi would have understood his native Austrian the better; only in the Legion it is mostly French, even very bad French, that is spoken.

Odd Skadshaim drifted up, seeing the

trouble on Joseph's face. He said: 'Old man, you are looking at death, are you not? I can see it in your face.'

Joseph's face relaxed a little at the quaintness of the expression, and then he said: 'Perhaps it is death that we are faced with, just as you said, Norje.' He sighed. 'In two days, many bad things have happened, Willi. It all seemed to begin with those Arabs who brought back parts of poor Pierre Planche. In two days we have lost two brave officers; today we have seen our third led to his quarters by a sergeant because he was too drunk to take command. It is making the men upset, and they are saying bad things about the lieutenant.'

Willi murmured loyally, '*Il n'est pas aussi diable qui'il est noir.*' (He is not as black as he is painted.)

But the more direct, less emotionally complicated Norwegian impatiently waved him into silence. 'Let us hear Joseph,' he said roughly. 'This is no time for the white-washing of incompetents, Willi. You have much to tell us, yes, Joseph?'

'Yes,' said Tillfru lugubriously. 'Too

much. There are men in the next room who are plotting — men like Tissdan and the bullying Fiertel. And Fiertel and Tissdan, Schweld and others are in there with them, and men of similar spirit from the other barrack rooms.'

'Plotting?' Willi sat up quickly.

Tillfru nodded so that his long moustaches swung with the movement. 'They have seen sergeants rise against a superior officer, and they are saying that if sergeants can do that, then should the occasion arise they too can rise against the sergeants.'

Willi and the Norwegian exchanged startled glances. 'But what does it all mean?'

Joseph said, simply: 'Listen!' In the distance they could hear Glik's savage voice shouting, to be followed by a quick cry of agony.

'Do you not understand? Those sergeants are swine, and Glik is the most brutal of the three. Without the need for restraint, can you not imagine what a hell they can make of our existence here in the fortress? And the men are frightened by the prospect, and they are already saying that they will have none of it. Already there is talk of revolt.'

'What?' Skadshaim jumped to his feet. 'Are they mad? Is this the time for disunity? Out there are thousands of Arabs, ready at any moment to launch an attack. Can we afford to have fighting among ourselves?'

Willi Pretel was off his bed in a moment, his face registering his alarm. Swiftly he fastened the belt that he had loosened before lying down to test. He said: '*Mon dieu*, we are almost leaderless as it is. Whom do those fools propose to have as leaders if they remove the Trinity?'

Joseph Tillfru said dryly: 'Fiertel will tell you, Fiertel. And Tissdan will tell you . . .'

'Tissdan.' Odd Skadshaim nodded cynically.

'And there are many Fiertels and Tissdans in these barrack rooms.'

Odd Skadshaim rapped: 'Yes, and who would want to have them as leaders in a battle against the Arabs?'

They looked at each other, concerned. Then Pretel said: 'We must do something, Norje. But what?'

* * *

There was darkness all over the desert after darkness had fallen. The fires of the encamped Arabs reflected in a red glow against the soft blue-black of the star-studded night sky — ominously those fires almost ringed the fortress completely now, as reinforcements trickled in to swell the main force.

Fortress El Zeeb threw a glow into the sky. Oil lamps were burning in every room and around the parade ground; the steady yellow glow fell on the sleeping faces of those legionnaires who had been relieved from guard on the wall — fully clothed, they lay there, rifles to their side. If there was to be a stand-to because of attack, there must be no confusion in the dark.

But somewhere within the fortress a man's eyes were open, and he was lying there, watching and waiting.

151

Shortly before midnight, Sergeant Glik, the Latvian, finished in the company office, yawned noisily and went out to seek his bed. The guard corporal, none other than the good Corporal Brissel, so soon forgotten as a hero that he was on guard again, saw him go.

Ten minutes later he saw him again.

But Legionnaire Henri Putôt saw him first.

They came out at his call, thinking that here was the expected attack. Every man, sergeants, corporals, and legionnaires. Not, of course, the white-faced lieutenant; and Sergeant Glik was already there.

When they saw The Paralysed One he was crouching his haunches rather like a dog, his head lifted, trying to force sound through his twisted face. Like a dog bays at the moon when there is death; only here was no moon just yet . . . but death, yes.

In the yellow lamplight of that sandy parade ground a man lay twisted in final agony. Sergeant Glik. When they examined him they saw that someone had knocked him down from behind and then passed a thin cord round his neck and put a knee in his back and pulled. There were marks on the ground to suggest that in his last moments the sergeant had fought frantically to save his life, and his fingers were torn and bleeding.

But he had died. The terror of the company lay in a grotesque contortion of limbs, his eyes bulging sightlessly, his steel teeth catching the yellow glint from the swinging oil lamps. For — and this is important — they were swinging gently now, as the breeze softly caught them . . .

It was the spark that started the flame, the assassination of the sergeant. The men were in a state of considerable tension even before it happened, but this touched them off.

Instantly the fortress was in an uproar. Men were shouting, getting ever more excited, more irrational . . . more stupid.

For, as Odd Skadshaim said, consider — here was the formidable, little-loved Sergeant Glik dead at their feet . . . a thing all men had asked to see . . . and what did those same men do now?

They shouted for revolt for an end to

all their leaders. And their argument? They were unfitted for their task, because they were allowing themselves to be killed off one by one!

'So they would hasten the process,' Odd said grimly, and he and Willi Pfetel and Joseph of the long moustache and men of similar spirit began to move together, away from the larger, wildly-talking throng.

It was illogical; but night is no time for dispassionate thought, not when you have been dragged from sleep in order to see the remains of a man done brutally if expertly to death. And that silent ring of fires all around the horizon did nothing to add to their comfort.

After a time, things began to crystallize. The hotheads and malcontents, as well as the weak-willed and excited, gathered together round a legionnaire from Poland who was known as Zac (though the card over his bed said he was Legionnaire Zacowski). Fiertel and Tissdan, he of the shaven skull, were there, and with them three-quarters of the legionnaires.

In another part of the parade ground

were the steadier, less excitable element, such as Pretel, Chopin, Tillfru, Skadshaim, Renard, Dupin, Voronex and Kierplé . . . but a tiny force compared with the others.

And then a third group of N.C.O.s stood together under the leadership of the savage Sergeant Zirko. Phare was with him, storming and raving, but that did no good because he couldn't be heard above the shouting of the rebellious group.

Only the English legionnaire, he who looked so unlike an Englishman, stood alone. He appeared to find it all very interesting.

The shouting went on, and with it the swirling movement of the larger, excited group of legionnaires. And then, in time, they began to turn and face the other parties, and then Zac came to the fore, flanked by others of like spirit.

He was a spare, grey, thin-faced man, a man who talked without letting you see his eyes . . . a troublemaker, who preferred to let others take the risks. But now he had made himself leader and he had to stand out and speak for his followers.

Phare started to jump forward, all fire and zeal, but Sergeant Zirko shoved him back with a growl. Zirko came after Glik in seniority, and he knew that Phare wasn't the man for a delicate situation like this.

He shouted, roughly: 'I've been calling you to attention and you have paid no heed. Be sure you will regret this tomorrow!'

A roar rose from the malcontents at that, the roar of a beast turned savage and wanting to strike back. It encouraged Zac, if he had been needing encouragement, that is.

He called back: 'Perhaps there will be no tomorrow for some people,' and then the shouting went up again, only it was pitched higher this time, and there was a rasp to the edges of the sound. Simultaneously, there was a little surging movement, as if the men would leap forward and complete the Pole's ironic prophecy right there and then.

And every man carried arms, because

he had been expecting an Arab attack — every man within those high walls carried a gun, and they were lifting to point at each other.

Big Willi Pretel watched it with horror. He was saying to himself, 'Oh, my God, what madness is this? Must we slay each other with the enemy ready to complete the business for us?'

He, too, took a step forward, though it was an involuntary gesture, and for some reason all his party closed in behind him.

On that yellow, lamp-lit parade ground it seemed as though the three parties were coming closer suddenly, determined to complete their madness and get to grips. Up on the ramparts the guards watched, and they were dividing mentally, each committing himself to one party or the other.

Zirko straddled with his legs wide apart. His voice thundered as if in tremendous anger, though inwardly he was cool and was calculating every movement from the rebels. 'What is this talk? Are you aware that this is the Legion and there is severe punishment for those who would usurp authority?'

Zac shouted back: 'Are you aware that soon there will be no authority in El Zeeb? Are we to stand like sheep and watch our leaders struck down one by one because they cannot keep away the Arab assassins?'

Emile Zirko was startled. So they thought that responsibility lay with the Arabs for these deaths . . . It was the sort of colourful theory that would find acceptance among the legionnaires.

'Fools,' he sneered. 'How could an Arab get in here and kill, as you think he is doing? Fools, do you not realise that the killer is one of us? The killer is somewhere here right now . . . '

'Then find him before it is your turn!' a voice shouted from the back. Another roar went up, a spiral of savage sound that must have been heard far across the desert by the silent Arabs, and caused them to wonder.

Willi Pretel made a decision at that moment. Without consulting his friends, he simply walked across and stood with the tiny party of N.C.O.s. Without hesitation, his followers came and joined him. The action roused Zac and his rebels to anger and they shouted despicable things at Willi and his friends, and for another moment there was a threat of guns being used.

Yet curiously — or perhaps because of it — the merging of the two tiny parties seemed to have a sobering effect. The anger died to a sullenness, and then the tenseness began to vanish and the parties ceased to watch each other with quite so much care. In time men even thought of sleep.

The rebels went back to their beds, but Sergeant Zirko restrained the legionnaires within his party when they began to follow, though they did so, assuredly, with reluctance and hesitation. He called them back: 'You will not be safe tonight among those wolves, *mes braves*. Tonight, my friends, we shall stay together here in the tower. The night is warm, and you will not miss your blankets.'

They made themselves comfortable, though they crowded the few habitable rooms in the tower. The two sergeants and some corporals bedded down in the chamber where two fort commanders had come to an untimely end.

But one of them could not sleep.

He was wondering why fate had chosen this time to attack their leaders, a time when they had two good sergeants back in hospital in Alfia, and only junior N.C.O.s to fill their place.

But more especially he was thinking about the lieutenant who was known as L'Irrité. The situation had changed. It had been big Glik who had ordered the lieutenant to be removed from the parade ground, big Glik who had poured the liquor down the lieutenant's throat. He, Sergeant Zirko, had merely been ordered to assist the 'sick' lieutenant to his quarters, and that, he was prepared to swear, was all that he had done.

If there had been trouble, he could have thrown all the blame on to Glik, the Latvian. Only now there was no Glik the Latvian, so that if there was trouble it was conceivable that he would have to bear it all himself.

Emile Zirko lay staring into the

darkness, thinking about all the trouble that could come to him — trouble simply because he had agreed with Glik that the lieutenant was incapable of conducting the defence of the fortress as circumstances demanded it should. It had seemed a sensible thing at the time to remove a raving, drunken lieutenant and put him to sleep out of harm's way until the attack was beaten off. But the attack had not come, and assuredly within hours the lieutenant would be awake and presumably no less a menace again. Zirko knew that with that formidable force patiently waiting to strike at them, they could not afford any folly from their leader; for folly would probably mean death to them all, and Zirko had no wish to die.

That was one thing. But another disturbing thought he had voiced before. What if L'Irrité had not been so far drunk that he could remember being forcibly filled up with strong alcohol? If he remembered that and reported the assault on him, then he, Sergeant Zirko, would spend an unhappy few years in a Penal

Battalion, if he escaped the wall, that is. And Zirko had caused too many to join the 'Zephyrs' to want to join them himself.

He was not a man to get involved emotionally with his thoughts, no matter what they were. He was able to lie in the darkness and think clearly of the issues at stake and come to a decision without so much as a quickening of the pulse. But before he arrived at a decision, he came to a conclusion. And that conclusion was that there was no danger to Sergeant Zirko except through the presence of Lieutenant L'Irrité. A decision followed naturally upon that conclusion, a decision that did not seem over-drastic because the sergeant knew that anyway in the next hours or days many of his comrades were doomed to die, if not all of them.

Before dawn, he rose silently and crept down the broad, stone steps and went across to the room where L'Irrité lay. He kept to the shadows and was sure that no sentry high up on the ramparts saw him go. But when he went into that silent, dark room, a man stood back in the distance and watched him.

And someone else watched the watcher . . .

10

The Sergeant Called Zirko

L'Irrité lay with the diffused light from the parade ground lamps upon his drawn white face. Emile Zirko stood over him, his face a mass of shadows with only the gleam of his eyeballs pricking out of the dark hollows. There was no emotion on his face; this was something that had to be done for the safety of Emile Zirko, so it would be done, quickly and without fuss. Compassion, sorrow, regret — what had they to do with it?

He took a bottle of cognac from the litter on the table and opened it. Then with a quick movement he held the lieutenant's nose for a second time, and when the mouth came open, suddenly he slopped in as much liquor as he could. The bottle he dropped to the floor; one hand still held the nose, the other flattened across the mouth and pressed

164

against the convulsive attempts to remove it.

You die in a minute or so, if your throat is full of burning liquor and all air is kept from your lungs. It also has the advantage of looking like death from overdrinking.

And that was how it looked when Zirko finally rose and took a drink from the bottle and then set it close by the limp white hand of the dead officer. A touch of artistry that would probably have met with the approval of his dead friend the Latvian if he could have seen it.

Then he went out, softly, closing the door behind him without sound. It was still dark, but there was a light suffusing the eastern horizon, and within minutes that impatient sun would be climbing over the rim of the desert.

And a man stood there before the sergeant. A smaller man, a man whose head was craned forward like that of an ugly, dry old tortoise. A man who said, 'What have you been doing?'

The man of God, Sergeant Etienne Phare, the pillar of rock, the beacon, the lighthouse to the world — at any rate, to the world of godless legionnaires.

Shoving his small, withered face into his, his eyes ablaze with suspicion. Demanding again, 'What have you been up to?'

Zirko recovered and said, so smoothly, 'I was anxious, concerned about the poor lieutenant. I came down to see that no harm had come to him.'

'And has there?' Quickly, like a rapier thrust.

And Zirko spread his hand. 'He was not used to drink. Drink and cafard did it. He must have died in the night . . . '

Phare's head came back, only now it wasn't like a tortoise's; it was like a cobra's, and it seemed ready to strike.

'Dead?' he said. His voice went higher. 'The lieutenant is dead?'

Suddenly Zirko found himself pushed aside and Sergeant Phare rushed into the room. Zirko waited at the door. He wanted to think. Things had gone wrong again . . .

Phare came back, slowly. He seemed to sidle round the doorpost, his eyes on Zirko. The light was getting stronger now, and Zirko could see the fanatical gleam in the older man's eyes.

Phare accused — 'He must have died in the night. You said so, didn't you? But why then is his body so warm that death must surely have come within minutes — within the time that I have been watching this building?'

Zirko lunged. He had to stop Phare's blabbing mouth. Fear now mounted within him. From a small action events had directed him into this position, where his own life was in serious threat. His one thought now was to take Phare by the throat and throttle him.

But Phare had a bayonet in his hand. It flashed up and pointed at his middle. Zirko flung himself backwards, out of reach.

Sergeant Phare began to shout, a great noise though few words were distinguishable. Zirko circled desperately for a moment, seeking a last opportunity to jump in and silence that clacking tongue. But Phare crouched, bayonet point following him, and all the time that small wrinkled mouth was open and shouting.

On an impulse, with no real thought in his mind, Zirko ran away. Swiftly he leapt up the steps to the tower, then stopped at the door without going in.

Men were stirring, coming out in great haste, sure that this time it was the call to arms. And day was coming up in a great blaze of yellow light, and another night had passed from every man's life.

They came pouring out of the doors of the barrack rooms, and were streaming out from the tower. Phare stood by the door of the officer's quarters, his bayonet pointing up the sun-tinged steps to where Zirko stood, a crowd of legionnaires thronging behind him.

Irresolute, the other force stood in a growing group across the parade ground. Earlier that morning Sergeant Phare had been an enemy; they suspected that here was some trick to put down their insurrection.

But Phare was shouting things that were incredible, appearing to have nothing to do with last night's affair . . .

He was shouting that Lieutenant L'Irrité was dead. That Lieutenant

L'Irrité had been murdered. That the murderer was — Sergeant Emile Zirko the Swiss!

They were astounded, but not incredulous. For any bizarre happening seemed not out of place in this crazy fortress of El Zeeb.

Zirko was cool again, thinking rapidly. And he knew what to say.

'You old fool, you are cafard!' he roared, as if in terrible anger. 'What is this that you are saying? Who says the lieutenant is dead? Why do you accuse me of a murder when I have just been wakened from sleep by your silly, shouting voice?'

Phare stood across in the middle of the parade ground now, his shadow long in the morning sun. He turned his small, weathered face that looked again like a malignant tortoise's up to where Zirko stood on the steps.

'By God, you lie,' he shouted in passion. 'Did I not see you with my own eyes enter this place but a few minutes ago? Did you not tell me yourself that the lieutenant was dead from drinking too much liquor? And on your breath was not there the smell of the brandy that you drank to steady your nerves after your foul crime?'

Zirko jumped forward a couple of steps, as if righteously stung to anger . . . and it kept his floating breath from betraying him to the crowding legionnaires.

'Oh, you babbling old man,' he cried. And then he played boldly. 'You have had a bad dream. We shall find that our lieutenant is not even dead at the end of all this. Come, you, Legionnaire Zac, and you Corporal Lechner, form you into a deputation to ask after the health of our commanding officer. And if he wakens and is angry, explain, if you please, that it is our Sergeant Phare who has the too vivid imagination.'

Corporal Lechner obediently pushed past him. Zirko held his breath. Suspiciously the Pole came across and the two went in together. Half a minute later both were back at the door. Zirko's voice rang out loud and confidently. 'Well?'

Corporal Lechner spread his hands.

'The lieutenant is dead.'

A murmuring rose on all sides at that. But Sergeant Phare's voice rang out and stilled it.

'The lieutenant has been struck down by a man of inferior rank. That is a crime against God. God wills that we hold the positions allotted to us, and man must not presume to act against divinely appointed authority.' And more like that — the babbling of a man who is a crank and an eccentric. He stood there and shouted all this, for all the world like a man touched with religion in the market place of any village in France — an ugly little man, even comical in his ill-fitting uniform. But dangerous, so dangerous for his brother sergeant.

Zirko made something like a mistake. He shouted, to quiet that accusing voice, 'You are imagining things, old man. This, clearly, is yet another crime by the assassin of Captain Paon, the lieutenant, and Sergeant Glik.' Incautiously he went too far. He shouted, 'The Arab assassin has struck again, undoubtedly!' Because that had been the theory that men had wanted to embrace last night, so that now it seemed policy to encourage and foster the belief.

Only, men are perverse. One moment they want to believe in something and will insist on believing even in the face of reason; the next they fly away from the theory just because there is apparent support for it. Men shifted and murmured, and then Zac's vague, grey face came round and he called, 'But last night you did not believe in Arab assassins, *mon sergent.*'

Swiftly Zirko recovered. 'Very well, then; if you won't have your Arab assassin this morning, let us embrace my theory of last night. *Someone among us is striking down our leaders!*' One by one they have gone!' He looked round keenly, then, a clever touch, said, 'It will be my turn next, you see; for am I now in command of this fortress, and has not each fort commander been struck down.' His voice lifted. 'Look every man among you. Think, for your neighbour might be the killer who is jeopardising the safety of us all!'

He was a very clever man with his tongue, Sergeant Emile Zirko.

But always there was little, crab-apple faced Phare, he of the fanatic theories, to upset him. Phare was pointing again with his bayonet, and now he was impatient for action.

'The killer of our last fort commander is you, Sergeant Zirko,' he shouted. 'Be sure there will be retribution for this crime against God and the Legion. I am assuming authority and order that you be put under arrest. Corporal of the guard, confine Sergeant Zirko where he can do no harm to himself or to us.'

Corporal Brissel looked unhappily from one sergeant to the other. He didn't know what to make of this. Then the decision was solved for him in an unexpected manner.

The tall, raw-boned English legionnaire, he without teeth in the front, strolled slowly, casually, between the two parties. He was pointing up at the flag, and there was a pleasant air of satisfaction about him.

'Look, my children,' he called. 'See the

flag of France. See how it stirs and sometimes even cracks like a whip. See, and understand what that might mean to us. For this is the time of the season of the winds, and if I am not misled by the signs, within hours we shall have a sandstorm blowing up against us. That, my friends, is why the Arabs are sitting quietly out in the desert. They are waiting for the wind to blow, so that the dust rises and they can attack without being too easily seen.'

That was all he said. He made a statement, but offered no counsel of advice. When he had finished he went to where he had leaned his rifle and without being ordered mounted to his battle position near to the gate.

Every man lifted his eyes to that tricolour, streaming before the wind. And every man knew that the Englishman who had fought under Kitchener was right.

No one said anything; no compromise was reached verbally. But every man went about his duties. The affair of the lieutenant who had justly earned the title of L'Irrité could be left for later solution.

The Norwegian had instantly started across to the wall, but a swift sharp, '*Halte!*' from Sergeant Emile Zirko stopped him. Zirko turned and looked back at the men who had been his followers a few minutes ago; they were coming down the steps from out the various rooms of the tower.

Zirko put up his hand, that hand which so recently had pressed out the life of his lieutenant. 'No, my friends,' he called softly. 'Let us not run our heads into the lion's mouth. Who is to say what will happen to us if we mingle with those rebellious dogs, who in their folly are jeopardising the safety of us all? Might they not suddenly act upon a plan and seize us all and wreak vengeance upon us because we opposed their craziness this last night? That Zac is a treacherous snake, I tell you.'

They stopped and looked across at the other, far larger party. Men were dispersing without being told, but in the middle of the dusty parade ground a knot of men walked more slowly away. They were talking — there was the grey-haired, grey-eyed, grey-faced Pole in the middle; Schulle, Tissdan, Le Groneau, Fiertel and other vicious men pressing in to hear; and in the middle, like a ruffled bantam cock, was Sergeant Etienne Phare.

It was too far away to hear what was being said, but there was something sinister in the manner of that little group. Here, one knew, was secret plotting, and it could only be directed at them.

Zac was steering the conversation. The split between the sergeants had been a heaven-sent opportunity to them. A moment ago they had been in a dangerous position whereby their actions could have been construed as mutiny — and undoubtedly would have been, before a tribunal of stiff-backed Legion officers across the desert in Alfia.

But now, here was Authority itself, the good Sergeant Phare, curse his guts, taking charge of their party and inciting them to action against the others. This was no longer mutiny; this was acting under the orders of a superior, and therefore right even in the eyes of the stiffest-backed colonel.

So they plotted, and the flag streamed out more boldly, and over the desert dust devils suddenly rose and spiralled and lived longer with each passing minute — higher they grew and more frequent, so that after a time it would have been difficult to distinguish a white-cloaked Arab from these dancing dust devils.

But this was still not the time for the expected attack. It would come soon after that yellow haze on the southwest horizon had spread towards them, that yellow curtain that was the forefront of a dust storm that could last for days, and which would put out the sun and bring night, almost, over the great Sahara desert around Fortress El Zeeb.

Zirko, he of the bad teeth and the evil heart, could see that distant, raging storm from a position on the steps of the tower. He spoke once again to his men.

'Let this be our plan,' he said. 'Those fools under the even more incredibly foolish Sergeant Phare, can defend the walls. We — our little but so-gallant party — will conduct the defence from the tower.' He paused, his dark eyes brooding as he looked once again at that advancing yellow storm. 'My children, they are very strong, these Arabs, and in great number. And they seem for once to be well led, as witness this not usual tactic of waiting for a storm to cover their movements. Truly they must be well led, for an Arab going to war is usually a most impatient fellow.

'That being so, we, a divided force, might be hard-pressed to keep them out. Therefore, I say, let us keep to the tower, so that if the fortress is overrun, we of the faithful heart will be together for the final defence.'

He was a man of flowery, flattering speech, this Swiss called Zirko. But though his followers were not in disagreement about staying together in the tower, there were some who called for other action, too.

A corporal named Ragrander stepped forward, sweating under his kepi because they had stood too long in the hot morning sun.

'*Mon sergent,*' he said, 'perhaps there is one among us who might escape to Alfia under cover of this thrice-cursed sand-storm and secure the relief that assuredly we shall need.'

Zirko nodded gravely. 'There is thought in that suggestion, *mon brave*,' he said. 'Perhaps it could be done. But who is there among us who might stand a chance of getting through the Arab lines?'

Big Willi Pretel was looking towards the gate just then, and his eyes alighted on the tall, rangy-framed Englishman. He turned. 'There,' he said, pointing, 'is the man for you, sergeant. He knows these Arabs, knows their ways better than any among us, and he can speak their language. If he could go out dressed as an Arab, and secure possession of a horse . . . '

Zirko cupped his hands and bellowed, 'Legionnaire Warr,' and Warr looked up, interested at once. Then he dropped down the face of the wall and came trotting over to the crowd on the steps.

Zirko said, '*Mon brave*, you have the honour of being selected for a desperate mission. It is unanimously agreed that you are the best qualified among us to cross the Arab lines under cover of this so-malignant sandstorm,' and he smiled kindly at the legionnaire.

Warr looked out over the fortress wall, his eyes thoughtful and yet still interested. When he spoke there was even pleasure in his voice. 'It will be an expedition of the most entrancing,' he said. 'And be sure, *mes amis*, I will not fail to get through. A horse is all I need — that I can assuredly get. In about four days I shall be back and with me a relieving force that will assuredly put those brave enemies of ours to flight.' And his manner seemed to suggest that he had regrets at the thought.

He began to go down the steps. Over his shoulder he called, 'I will make me a *galabier* and cloak, such as the Arabs wear. And I have a sword and knives that are good and sufficient, for were they not made by Arabs?' Then he paused curiously and amended thoughtfully, 'No, not a sword.'

Then he went, and when the first swirling yellow dust cloud came rolling over the fortress wall, they opened the gates for an instant and he slipped out, a legionnaire but indistinguishable from an

Arab in his hooded cloak ... a legionnaire but almost an Arab in his ways and outlook and sympathies.

And Willi Pretel, lying with his rifle butt against his cheek, peering through a loophole in an upstairs room of the tower, a room immediately below that in which two deaths had swiftly occurred, looked after him and his mind was troubled.

For, he thought, could it not be that this mad Englishman might have been the assassin who had demoralised the garrison with his killings? Le Legionnaire Warr could quite conceivably have fitted the role, and now they were encouraging him to leave them ...

11

The Attack Begins

Zirko was a good sergeant who knew his business, that at least could be said in favour of the man. All the doors and windows on the ground floor of the tower were barricaded; in the lower rooms men were posted with food and drink and a sufficiency of ammunition to withstand a siege. Unfortunately there was no way of getting from the bottom to the higher floors in the tower, except by coming outside and mounting the flight of stone steps. That was yet another defence measure, to make the upper floors as near as possible impregnable.

Willi Pretel and a dozen N.C.O.s and men were on the floor above, and above them a similar number in the death chamber and adjoining small rooms. And above all, four men with rifles and three men with the clumsy machine gun kept watch from right on top of the tower. Zirko watched them climb the steel ladder to take up positions, then passed up food and water containers and boxes of ammunition. He saw them safely installed, and the trap lowered after them, and then went on his rounds to inspect the other defences. He was a thorough man, Sergeant Zirko, but then he knew their lives might depend on his thoroughness.

And outside, high up on the wall defences, Zac was murmuring to Fiertel, Schulle and Jopin, 'There are so many, my friends — too many, I think. And when this storm reaches us, we shall not see them until their scaling ladders are hooked on to the wall and they are mounting up towards us. Then, perhaps, it will be too late.'

He looked across the desert to where the main Arab encampment lay. The rising wind had whipped the dust up from the desert and made a screen between them so that now there was nothing to be seen. In half an hour the full force of the storm would be upon them, and then it would be almost as night and conditions would be ideal for the attacking force. It was not a cheering sight for the defenders, that rising, swirling blanket of dust.

Jopin carefully dug the accumulating sand from the inner corners of his eyes and said, 'And what would you have, my friend?' Because he knew that the Pole had some plan in mind or he would not have spoken thus.

Zac looked round carefully before speaking. His voice low, he said, 'Under the circumstances it would be as well for us to consider our own safety. Not immediately, that is, but should the fighting go hard with us — why, a man should consider all these things.'

Fiertel slid down so that his face was protected a little against the needling grains of sand that the wind was whipping up. He was crude and direct.

'Out with it, you cunning dog,' he said brutally. 'What is there on your mind that you want us to know?'

So Zac told them. It was bad that a garrison should be divided among itself, as was this at El Zeeb. That meant a weakening of resistance, and the enemy was strong. And the manoeuvring of Sergeant Zirko had not escaped him, either.

'See, Zirko has kept his men to the tower and is busy fortifying it. That I had not expected. That means that we poor legionnaires must bear the brunt of the battle along the walls and at the gate, and if we are overrun, why, we die out here because the tower will be barricaded against us just as much as the Arabs.'

Fiertel and the others were silent, looking across at the squat tower with its tricolour now streaming at full length in the haze above. This they had not thought of. But Zac had, and he had thought beyond it, too.

'We will stay — it is better thus — while ever there is a chance of defending the fortress. But should it become obvious that we cannot maintain our position, then . . . '

He spoke rapidly for a few minutes. When he had finished his friends nodded in satisfaction, and then went and told their friends along the wall, so that in time only Sergeant Etienne Phare was in ignorance of the plot.

By midday the storm was fully upon them, and then life was truly wretched for the men who had to watch out and face it. The sand hurt as it scoured into their unprotected flesh, and it powdered their eyebrows and weighted down their eyelashes and covered them from head to foot in a fine grey-white coat. It got up their nostrils so that in time they were blocked and had to be prodded clear, and always it was in their mouths, grating between their teeth, gritty to the tongue as it moved in their dry mouths.

For no matter how much they drank, always they felt dry and thirsty. So dry were they because of the hot, moisture-lacking wind that their fingers were wrinkled like the surface of old gloves, and the skin on their bodies felt detached and dead and seemed to belong to someone else.

Truly it was the hour of their misery and discomfort.

And the Arabs did not attack.

About four in the afternoon Sergeant Zirko, as unremitting as ever, came down to where Pretel, the Norwegian, Dalarge and others lay in huddled wretchedness against the loopholes.

'They do not come, *mon sergent*,' said old JosephTillfru, and his voice seemed peevish, as though he were complaining.

Zirko laughed and clapped the old man affectionately on the shoulder. 'What there, my impatient old fire-eater. You are not afraid of these Arabs, *hein?*' And because he knew it was good for morale and he was a good sergeant, he called attention to the situation and exclaimed delightedly, 'A few wretched Arabs — it will take more than that to scare him, the good Joseph, eh? — *Il en a vu bien d'autres . . .* '

They smiled. The strength that was inside that evil man yet filled them so that they were the better soldiers. And then they looked out of their loopholes into the yellow pall that drove in fury upon the exposed desert fortress.

Pretel sighed and said, 'It is to our advantage, always provided that the

Englishman was successful in stealing a horse from the Arabs and getting safely through their lines. The longer they are in starting an attack, the less defending we shall have to do before the relief comes.'

Zirko laughed again and said, 'That is so, my friend,' and went out again. But on the steps he paused to look over the dim outline of the fortress wall, with its huddled defenders crouching by the rifle slits.

They were in no state to put up maximum resistance to the Arabs, with the garrison divided among itself as it was. The situation was fantastic, he swore. Two separate parties conducting separate defences of the fortress, and neither trusting each other, even to mixing together. It was an incredible situation.

And then the lines furrowed on his forehead again, because there was a thought deep in his mind that had been insisting to be believed and he didn't want to believe it. Now it came again.

Was there something in that wild theory that kept springing up within the garrison that the murderer of their leaders was an Arab? He narrowed his eyes against the driving fury of dust and sand and tried not to believe it, tried not to think of it, and failed.

He found himself suddenly awash with theories and speculations, as though he were some legionnaire with the too-vivid imagination, like that little, wild-talking man who caused so much trouble, the Legionnaire Chopin.

Suppose there was something in the theory? Suppose that this time these Arabs were displaying more cunning than they had ever shown before? Suppose that it had all been a deliberate plan, not only to deprive them of the leaders they would need when the big attack came, but also, by the very way in which it was done, it had been intended to rot the morale of the legionnaires in advance?

He tried not to believe in it — the plan seemed too extraordinarily deep for it to have been conceived that way — but part of his mind was wanting to believe in the fantasy.

For wasn't that the way it had happened, wasn't that the way things had turned out to be?

It was incredible. But then the whole affair was incredible, unbelievable. Perhaps the most incredible, unbelievable thing about it all being that one tiny circumstance after another had led him, Sergeant Emile Zirko, into smothering out the life of a weakling officer. That was inconceivable, or would have been but a few days before, when the good Captain Paon had held them together as a good officer, however old and withered and dried and sticklike, can . . .

Zirko abruptly switched his thoughts from the uncomfortable one concerning the abrupt decease of the white-faced lieutenant. He did not want to think of that. Instead he speculated once again upon the story that had come to the sergeants, of a night recently when, so it was said, Captain Paon had ordered the gate to be unbarred and a mysterious thing had happened. The gate had partly opened, after a long time, and then quietly closed. That was all.

But next day the fortress was full of the

rumour that the Arabs were massing for attack.

Zirko shook his head. All that he could not understand. It was a pity that he had not thought to question the lieutenant who had been with Captain Paon — perhaps L'Irrité, drunk, might have explained the mystery for him.

He began to mount the steps. He was thinking, 'If the mad Englishman gets through, it will still be four days before relief reaches us — perhaps longer, four days! *Ma foi!* Can we hold out that long, the way things are inside this fortress?'

He looked up at the fluttering flag, saw the nose of the machine gun protruding slightly through an embrasure and thought, 'Even if the fortress is captured, and that God-speaking Phare and his scum are put to the sword, this fortress will hold out until help comes, of that I swear!' And he patted the stout wall affectionately . . .

Something spanged against the tower, higher above his head, and then he heard the sound of the rifle crack out. Someone had fired at him, was his instant thought . . .

191

But the attack had started, though for a moment he didn't know it.

Suddenly, on all sides of the fortress, out of the enveloping storm had emerged a silent horde of Arabs. The wind was tearing at their gowns and cloaks, as if intent on unclothing them, but, inured to desert hardships, they paid little heed to it.

One moment only a blinding yellow storm raged against the stout fortress walls; the next a thousand Arabs were underneath and behind them a thousand more, and still more behind those. Zac saw them. His brain raced with lightning rapidity. On an instant, covered by the storm, he wheeled and fired at the back of Sergeant Zirko, dimly to be seen on the broad steps of the tower. Zirko was a man best out of the way if he, Zac, survived this conflict. But he missed.

Zirko rushed inside the tower and crashed the heavy door to. 'Now, my children,' he said gently, 'you see why Papa Zirko said, 'Let us not fraternise with that scum'. Assuredly some of us would not have lived if we had done.'

A hundred scaling ladders were on the wall, a hundred Arabs nimbly climbing. It meant that the defenders had to lean forward and expose themselves in order to shoot them down, and on the desert itself the ancient guns of the Arabs cracked out at every head and men died everywhere along that broad, strong wall.

Truly it was a clever plan, this attack of the Arabs.

Andre Gultos, the Belgian known as *Le Femme*, was among the first to die. His rifle was lifting but unfired, when some home made leaden bullet tore between his eyes and he pitched screaming forward so that he overhung the desert and yet didn't fall.

Then the little Chopin died and fell clean out over the wall, and because his limbs twitched in reflex when he landed they thought that he still lived and a dozen Arabs hacked him to such small pieces that there was no doubt then about the continued earthly existence of le Legionnaire Chopin.

Marcel Corroyer died, too, he of the earthly, corpse-like appearance and the unclean smell, but he did not die right away. Only when there were six or eight bullets lodged in his body did he slide down and bleed away and die.

And others died, so many others. But not Zac, and not Tissdan, Fiertel, Jopin, Schweld, Schulle and some others. They let others lean forward and take the risks and fight against that first wave; they wanted to live and they had a plan that could help them in that direction. So they kept well under cover and fired only at the more distant, shadow shapes farther out on the desert.

From the tower there was little that could be done to help the defenders on the wall. That was the evil of the situation. Because of the distance, only when the swirling dust storm cleared could the tower defenders see the Arabs spilling out there on the desert. Only in such intervals did their rifles crack out and give some assistance to the hard-pressed fighters on the ramparts. Sometimes the machine gun also chattered venomously for a few seconds, but it was badly sited, especially during this sandstorm, and great care had to be taken lest its bullets fell too low and struck their own men on the wall.

Suddenly Zirko, peering through the shuttered window, caught a glimpse of cavalry waiting beyond the main gate and divined the tactics. Swiftly he mounted the steel ladder and tried to lift the trap door. It seemed to be stuck. He hammered. After a while he was heard and the trap lifted and a legionnaire looked down.

Zirko, clinging to the steps, shouted, 'God in heaven, why do you bolt that trap door like that?'

But the man only looked surprised and said, 'We did not bolt it, *mon sergent*. In the movement one of us must have kicked the bolt, and it needs but to be a fraction across for it to lock the trap.'

But this was no time for petty explanations, though normally Sergeant Zirko would have delighted in making a lot about the accident. Instead he shouted, 'Keep watch on the gate. Out there in the storm the whole cavalry waits. Clearly it is expected that some

Arabs will enter the fortress, unlock the main gate and let in the cavalry. So, *mes braves*, watch out for the manoeuvre. Train all your guns on the gate and shoot down the dogs as they try to get in.'

He descended. The trap closed behind him. Above was the scuffle of feet as the heavy machine gun was manoeuvred into position. He went back to his post, and now he watched the more sharply the threatened position at the big gate.

The Arabs were no longer silent. No longer was it necessary. They came mounting the walls in wave after wave, screaming their war cries — '*Allah o akbah!*'

And now the sound of rifle-fire was incessant. Shots cascaded into a rain of harsh, crackling sound, and everywhere men died, sometimes silently, sometimes at length and with a pain that tore the voice out of them until they lay still forever more. And sometimes in this madness between men and men, the dying called on their god to avenge them, and the voices were French and German, Italian, Spanish, Hungarian and all the tongues of Europe. And sometimes it was an Arab cry, yet the god for all to whom they appealed was the same deity . . .

Hard by the gate an Arab headdress suddenly appeared, only to disappear as a bayonet drove into the face. But a second later there was another in his place, and other swarthy features were showing at different points along this section of the wall.

Back they were driven, only for more screaming fanatical Arabs to flood over in a fury that would not be denied, so that suddenly there were fifty or a hundred coming over the wall, with the defenders at this point falling butchered at their feet.

Instantly there was alarm throughout the fortress. The danger was apparent. If these Arabs could but open the gates, then a horde would come flooding in and the fight would be over in very short time, at least for a majority of the defenders.

Then the machine gun on top of the tower started up its rhythmic chattering and hot lead spewed viciously down towards the Arabs. In thirty seconds half were tumbling off the wall, dying; in a minute only two or three were alive. Few seconds later only dead Arabs remained inside the fortress.

The fight seemed to stop at that. It was as though some intelligent Arab chieftain outside said, 'Hold this slaughter. Here is a problem for us to consider unexpectedly. They have a machine gun, and they know how to use it.'

So they went back into the sandstorm, those Arabs, and the desert was silent now save for the moan of that wind that filled the sky with blinding yellow dust.

For a time no one moved, expecting the attack to be resumed at any moment. And then men relaxed and reached for their bottles of water, and some even ate the biscuits that were by their side. It seemed that the fight had been called off, for the moment at any rate.

Zirco went round the defences of the tower, heartening the men and encouraging them with extravagant praise. Unlike the defenders on the wall, there had been no casualties within the thick-walled tower. And the action had stirred them, so that they were in good spirits even without the flattery of their sergeant.

Out on the wall the atmosphere was not the same. Too many men had died in that first attack. Probably a third lay silent where they had fallen. And the men knew that another attack was bound to come. Perhaps they had won the first bout, but there was bound to be another, and if they won that — well, these Arabs always came back while they were in sufficient strength and out there they had an army.

So Zac spoke again to his men, and in a short time they had come to agreement. A few dropped on to the parade ground and went over and examined the fallen Arabs. There was looting, of course, and that was to be expected; for what need had these dead Arabs of the fine rings some wore and the delicate silver filigree brooches? And they even stripped the better-dressed of their fine robes and took them away with them.

And Zirko saw it all and didn't understand . . .

12

The Fatal Tricolour

Old Joseph Tillfru had a watch, a big, old-fashioned thing that had been made in Bavaria. He had looked at it only a few seconds before the engagement started, and it had read ten minutes past four. Now, when the Arabs had dissolved in the swirling dust, he looked again. Eighteen minutes past . . .

Truly many men can die in a very short space of time.

Zirko was aware of the shortness of the battle, and equally he was aware that in the three hours left of daylight, another and even more formidable attack might — would — probably be mounted. An engagement such as this could be all over in fifteen minutes.

He cursed the yellow fog that reduced the effectiveness of the massive fortress to such an extent. It was far worse than night, which would be too dark. And he cursed the circumstances that had led to the weakening of the defence in such a manner. That assassin — Arab or European — had much to answer for.

He was a good soldier, and for a bad man he was a very brave one. He would fight, but he knew that the odds were far too great against them — this combination of a large and intelligently led force and malignant nature with her blinding yellow dust storm would prove too much in time. That he knew. What he didn't know was — how long had the garrison to hold out before relief came?

With it all he retained hope. They had suffered much their first engagement, but see, had they not driven off the Arabs in the end? And was it not probable that they would, in spite of their leaderless, divided condition, defeat the next attack and perhaps the attack after that?

And always they would be gaining time with their victories, time during which relief would surely be speeding nearer.

'Be of stout heart,' he told his men when he returned to his post in the chamber where first Paon and the Le Gros had met their deaths, 'If we have courage, we will keep the dogs at bay until the Alfia garrison reaches us.'

Corporal Brissel, sometimes an optimist, added, 'Why, yes, and the dust storm might depart, and then, voila, is not our fortress as stout and unassailable as ever?'

Everyone cheered for a moment at the thought, and it was only on later reflection that they discounted this optimism considerably. These storms could rage for a week or more, and this one seemed assuredly set in for several days. Normally an Arab hated to fight or even to come out into the dust storm, but if they could be kept at it, as with their first attack, the outlook was not very favourable. Truly these Arabs must have found a very strong and unusually capable leader to force them into a fight under these conditions.

That Arab leader was unusual . . .

Within half an hour of the first attack, suddenly a new one developed. But this began with strange tactics. From beyond the gate, out in the swirling murk, suddenly a fierce barrage of rifle fire took up. The flashes were distinguishable, but the Arabs in their flowing robes were hardly to be seen.

The defenders on the wall nearest the Arabs opened fire at once and must have done much damage, and the Lebels in the tower also opened up, but the targets were harder to see.

Then a line of hidden Arab marksmen poured lead at the defenders along the ramparts, protecting the first party with their covering fire. The tactics had been very nicely worked out, indeed.

Zirko didn't understand them at all for many minutes. All he knew was that the opening fire had all seemed to be directed towards the tower, and even now bullets were whining upwards, to ricochet off with a frenzied screech into the yellow fog. He didn't understand it until too late.

A minute after the first crash of rifle fire, and the big attack developed anew.

Suddenly Arabs came racing as before out of the sandstorm. Heads wrapped in cloths to protect their faces from the storm, they ran forward with their scaling ladders. The legionnaires rose behind the ramparts to shoot viciously down upon their unprotected heads, but instantly a volley of rifle fire rose up from behind the first wave, and the slaughter was terrible.

El Zeeb was a fine fortress under normal conditions, sited so that an enemy must traverse open ground for at least half a mile in any direction before gaining the walls. But this awful yellow storm, that blinded the eyes and filled the lungs with gritty matter, reduced the effectiveness of the original planning. Now the conditions were as favourable to the attackers as to the attacked.

The Arabs were able to approach within fifty yards without being detected, sometimes even much closer. And an Arab could lie at that range and hardly be seen in the sand and yet be able to see quite dearly the heads of the defenders as they crouched up on the walls with their Lebels against their shoulders.

So, this wise Arab leader was sending in his storming force, while a circle of crouching Arabs on the fringe of visibility crashed in volley after volley of covering fire. Within seconds a legionnaire could not expose himself to shoot down at the storming party without himself being shot and put out of action.

They came on, a flood of wild, screaming men, wave after wave of be-gowned and colourfully robed Arabs, racing for the ladders that the first men were already hooking on the walls.

Sergeant Phare was roaring along the ramparts. He saw the situation. With this fog a man couldn't expose himself to the Arabs outside. Better that a man should wait until he saw them come over the top, or try to knock their ladders down.

He shouted these instructions, and to encourage them he shouted a reminder that behind was a machine gun that would surely wipe out any heathen Arabs that got over the wall. He also shouted that these Arabs deserved all they got, because were they not challenging the authority set over them, namely the over-lordship of their beloved France?

For Phare, he whose name meant

lighthouse, believed in such things and even in times like these it seemed urgent that others should understand and share his belief because that way he felt they would become stouter fighters.

The iron-hooked poles with their crude side steps clanged on top of the wall. Legionnaires stood back, butts hammering frantically at the weighted things; and sometimes a hook would slip and the ladder and all it bore would sway backwards and crash to the ground, its human freight screaming with horror at the approach of pain and smashed limbs and possibly death.

Ladder after ladder crashed backwards, only to be swiftly picked up and hoisted into position and a new wave of attackers start to mount it.

Sometimes it proved impossible to dislodge the hook — that was when weight of the ascending Arabs dug it too deeply into the wall. And then the fierce, yelling turbaned heads would mount up out of the yellow swirling fog, swords and knives would flash and cut and old fashioned, curiously carved pistols would suddenly, viciously discharge into a legionnaire's chest.

The legionnaires, standing back, would fire their Lebels straight into those faces, and blood would come and the yelling would cease and the Arab would seem to stand irresolute out in space and then go keeling backwards and fall. Sometimes the dead Arab would sweep all his clinging comrades off the pole, like a thumbnail swiftly detaching ripened ears of corn from a stalk, or a hand scooping winter-dulled flies from off a cord.

But always more mounted, always they came on. And sometimes they came so thickly that in time the Lebels were empty and there was no time to reload, and then again they were reversed and butts dug savagely at the mounting, shouting faces.

Then a lean Arab arm would reach out and catch the rifle before it could be drawn back, and the skinny arm would cling with incredible strength, immobilising the weapon until a fellow attacker could leap screaming from alongside and put an end to the legionnaire with a sharp, curved knife.

It was then that the force in the tower came into their own. Their rifles cracked like summer lightning, and in the moment of triumph the victorious Arab would totter, sag, and then pitch headlong on to the parade ground, dead or dying.

They fired until the building reeked of explosive, and their faces were blackened by smoke and the barrels of their Lebels were hot to the touch.

But now they too were losing men, at any rate in the upper quarters, where they were exposed to the Arab fire from beyond the wall. In time they began to realise that out there was a special squad of Arab marksmen who were directing their fire against them in the tower.

Old Joseph Tillfru died suddenly, abruptly, at a time when his Bavarian watch recorded nine minutes past five. Then Corporal Brissel staggered back with the blood flowing from under his chin and curious sounds clacking from his mouth; he died, but he was longer in going out and it was distressing because he was a good N.C.O. and a brave man.

Others died, too, and others were so terribly wounded that they needed medical attention quickly or they would follow their comrades. Among these was little Albert Volin, who had been born to the gutters of Paris and had learned that there are higher things in life than picking pockets.

Sergeant Zirko went his rounds with a rifle in his hand. One moment encouraging his men, the next snarling and showing those bad teeth and snapping off a shot through a loophole.

And all the time he was wondering how much longer they could last out, how much more these Arabs could suffer without giving up the fight. For assuredly if they kept up this intensity of attack they were bound in the end to overpower the wall defenders and flood in and open the gates for their cavalry, and then it was the end. Perhaps a few hours longer they might hold out up in this tower, but not much more than that.

A few hours . . . And they needed a respite of a few days if they were to hold the fort until the relief column arrived!

He looked out into the swirling yellow storm and wondered how far the English legionnaire had got on his mission. With luck, if he had succeeded in stealing a horse, he might be twenty or thirty miles on his way to Alfia.

Twenty or thirty miles! He found himself making a silent contemptuous movement with his hands. What good was that to them? If these Arabs kept on, they would have complete possession of the fortress long before the mad Englishman ever reached Alfia, much less a relief column march all the way back to them.

And perhaps the Englishman hadn't got through the Arab lines at that!

He ducked out of the door halfway up the stone flight of steps, and crawled swiftly up under cover of the thick wall. Lead screamed murderously over him, to end with a spurt of dust and a soggy little sound against the thick wall of the tower. Those Arabs out there were pouring bullets at the defenders in the tower as if their lives depended on it.

Pausing on all fours just by the door that led to the former commander's quarters, Sergeant Zirko found himself thinking of this leader the Arabs must have found. In this battle he had displayed exceptional resource, a brilliance that was unusual in desert warfare. So far, nothing he had done had been without reason.

Ziko found himself wondering at this tremendous barrage of fire that was directed against the tower defenders, wondering why the first shots of this second attack had all been hurled at the second line of defence, that is; the tower. Why? Why not concentrate fire on breaching the first line of defence — the wall — and then concentrate on the inner position? That was more orthodox tactics.

Zirko suddenly squatted on his haunches, kepi swirling in the driving, sand-laden wind, and squinted up to where the flag of France showed like a colourless rag in the dust storm. Suddenly he was very uneasy, suddenly he wanted to find an answer to an apparent inconsistency.

From the beginning of this attack, fire had been concentrated on the tower. Zirko thought, 'This fire-power would have been better employed directed against the legionnaires on the ramparts.'

And that was where the inconsistency arose.

Because during this battle the Arab leader had done nothing needlessly; therefore it suggested that there was a deep policy behind this ceaseless rain of bullets against the tower . . .

And Zirko suddenly understood.

Suddenly he realised that the machine gun was silent. Suddenly he realised that he had heard no answering fire to the barrage from the rooftop for quite some time.

With an oath he kicked savagely at the door, until it was opened and he could slip in. His face was streaming rivulets of sweat through the caking dust; his eyes glowed like near-black balls of fire in the dead-grey of his powdered face.

Suddenly he knew, he understood, and he was frantic with himself for not having seen the danger before.

That first attack had been defeated because unexpectedly the machine gun had mown down that flood of Arabs who had dropped within the fortress. That clever Arab leader had called his men off to consider the situation; for in those days the machine gun was not always to be found in the defence of a French Foreign Legion post. He must have realised that with a machine gun sited on the tower it would be almost impossible for his attackers to get within the fort and open up the gate to his hordes.

'So . . . he pours such fire on it that he keeps it out of action.' These were the tactics, that was why there was this incessant hail of lead upon the tower defenders.

'The machine gun is silent,' shouted Zirko above the din of firing. 'Perhaps we shall find our gallant comrades above have all been killed.' He started to climb the steel ladder, then paused to look within the main room. His force was suffering considerably now and was much depleted.

'Corporal Tusin, you, and half a dozen legionnaires will take the place of your comrades on the roof. That will leave us weak here. You, Corporal Dreifeld, will bring up all the men from the floor below — but not from the ground floor.'

Oh, no, not from the ground floor. They must stay behind their barricades and fight until not a man was left alive; for if the Arabs could secure entry they would set fire to the tower and roast the occupants alive. Oh, no, that was no way to fight the savage Arab!

Corporal Dreifeld scurried out to bring up Willi Pretel and his comrades. Tusin and his legionnaires prepared to follow the sergeant up the ladder.

He mounted swiftly and pressed on the trap door. It did not budge. He put his shoulder to it and heaved, and it moved not a fraction. Then frantically he hammered on it and called to the men at the top, as he had done before. But this time no one came to lift the trap, this time it remained firmly closed. There were no men alive now on the roof to open it for him.

Below the corporal and his men grew concerned. 'What is it?' rapped Tusin.

Sergeant Zirko looked down with savage face, sweat streaming from his exertion in that heat close by the ceiling. 'It has happened again!' In his mind he had a vision of those massive bolts that were fixed to the side of the trap. 'Somehow someone must have kicked against a bolt and knocked it across this thrice-cursed trap.' And then he stood and cursed clumsy legionnaires, stupid bolts and hostile, malignant traps.

Because in a moment he saw that whatever the circumstance, that trap kept them from their most valuable weapon, a weapon worth half a company of men alone. In a moment his hopes of holding out until that far-distant relief came blasted out of his mind. Without that gun, with their forces in such a divided, leaderless state — with this blinding storm and a brilliant Arab leader against them, they hadn't a hope of maintaining their defence for long.

Just then the door slammed back, and like big, awkward crabs, Willi Pretel, the Norwegian, Lacolle, Dalarge, and two or three corporals came scrambling in. Dreifeld shut the door and dropped the massive siege bolts into their sockets.

They rose, breathless, and then the bitterness that permeated this group around the ladder seemed to touch them.

Corporal Dreifeld wiped the dust from his hands by the simple process of rubbing them on his faded blue tunic. He said, quickly, anxiously, 'There is something wrong, yes?'

Zirko let his breath go in a long sigh and slowly, wearily descended. 'There is a lot wrong, *mon brave*. There is, in fact, everything wrong. Behold, within inches of us is our so valuable machine gun and we cannot get to it.'

'Cannot . . . ?'

Zirko shrugged, 'Above, all our comrades are dead, but before dying somehow in the movement someone must have knocked that loose bolt across and secured the trap against us. *Ma foi*, an accident, I know, but good God, that such an accident should have happened at this time! Yet we should have known, because did it not happen only a few hours before, and we failed to learn from the happening.'

He stood with his back to the ladder, his face tragic for a second, but then it hardened into a mask of fighting hatred. 'It is a blow,' he stormed, 'but we will show these Arabs how to die. By God, we'll fight to the last, and pretend we never had a machine gun!'

He was moving quickly into the main room, the others following. Only one man stayed and looked up at that massive trap door. A bandaged hand crept up to a nervous, twitching face, and the eyes that burned above spoke truly of the cafard that now crawled in his fevered brain.

Zirko heard his name. 'Sergeant Zirko.' He stopped and turned. 'I can get on to the roof and open up the trap to you. I can do it, because I have done it before — twice.'

It was the legionnaire called Sebastian Dalarge, he whose parents had been godly and had thrust him for their sins among rats of incredible size and ferocity, and thereby caused their son to become endowed with a special quality — a quality he would now demonstrate. An ability to defy this accidental bolt across a massive trapdoor.

Those bandaged hands were trembling as the sergeant looked at him, suddenly understanding. Hands that would need bandaging again within a short time . . .

13

The Treachery of Legionnaire Zac

It was just at this time that the fury of the attack seemed suddenly to mount with yet greater ferocity. As if some vigilant Arab leader had detected the significance of the silent machine gun on top of the tower, as if he was riding out there among his followers and in the name of Allah invoking them to yet greater efforts.

'This time, this time,' he would be saying. 'Victory is ours. Go, you sons of the desert, and show these Franks what fighting is.'

Now the tide was irresistible. Especially near to the big gate was the shock of the attack the greatest. Fanatically the Arabs swarmed over the parapet, hacking down the defenders and then dropping to the body-strewn parade ground and starting to run towards the gate. They died, because from the tower the defenders were merciless in their fire; and it was as though snow had fallen on a hot plate, the way the movement suddenly collapsed and died and seemed to shrink into the sand.

Even then, even without the machine gun, the defenders might have kept the Arabs away from the vital gate. For there is a limit to the slaughter that men will face, and these brave Arabs must have been near to it now. Perhaps even at that moment, there was in their hearts the thought that this was too much, that it would be better to flee and live, and submit to tyranny no less than before.

But man cannot see into the minds of men, and there were those among the defenders along the wall who saw in this flood of Arab attackers a quality of superhuman endurance that never ever exists in men. To some it seemed that these Arabs would never give in now that they had found a way over the wall; to some it seemed that it was only a matter of minutes before the gate opened and a great flood came to engulf them.

They were leaderless men, and that

explains the treachery that followed. It is the reason why men must have leaders; why they rot and go to pieces if there is no brain to control and coordinate their efforts and sustain them in morale.

For without leaders, men think of themselves, and thinking thus they bring trouble upon all around them, and even in the end so often upon themselves.

Zac did now. To Zac, with no confidence in this diminished force, denuded of officers, it seemed only a question of time before the end came for them all, and Zac thought that for a few of them there was a possible way of saving their skins. True he fought well and gallantly and did not behave selfishly while ever it seemed that the fortress would hold. But ahead of time he interpreted the signs to mean that Fortress El Zeeb had had its hour and was done.

So he spoke to Tissdan of the scarred and shaven skull and then to Fiertel and a few like friends of his, about a dozen or fifteen in all. And then on a signal they acted.

It was the defenders on the ground floor in the offices of the tower who first realised that something was wrong on the south wall. Suddenly, all too suddenly, it seemed that a breach had been made in the defences; suddenly they were all Arabs up top, and some of the Arabs were falling in their haste out on to the parade ground.

All in one moment it seemed that a tide flowed over the full length of the south wall, a tide of screaming gown-flapping, turban-headed desert warriors who flooded the parade ground and streamed in irresistible mass towards the great gate that alone kept out the main force.

It was massacre. Arabs died, as Arabs must, within the storm of lead from the defenders with their Lebels in the tower. But the legionnaires on the ramparts died, too, because now the attack was from within as well as from the ladders clinging to the outside of the wall. Horrified, their comrades in the tower saw one blue-coated legionnaire after another come toppling from the ramparts, screaming in death agony from some blow with a sword or sharp knife or a wound from a clumsy old pistol.

They saw that stringy-necked, tortoise headed little sergeant who believed so much in the divine right of those born to command — he was in the middle of the parade ground, shouting something that no one ever heard, a pistol that had been Le Gros's emptying into the victory-inflamed mob that came to tear him limb from limb, as they did a few seconds later.

And then the gate was swinging open, and the Arab cavalry came streaming in, and there was no machine gun to mow down the men who unfastened those bolts or the mounted Arabs as they raced into the fortress.

But it did one thing, and Zirko, standing at the door leading out on to the tower steps, was quick to recognise it.

It seemed like victory to the Arabs outside, and now they too came streaming in for the loot and the kill that their comrades were assuredly enjoying. For a moment the barrage of fire that rendered Dalarge's promise impossible, ceased.

Zirko said, brutally, 'Go, Dalarge.

Perhaps you will gain the roof before these excited warriors see you.'

Dalarge slipped out. Zirko slammed the door behind him and dropped the siege bolts again. If Dalarge failed, he wouldn't come back through that door.

Dalarge, he who was short but strong in the shoulders, crouched under the wall by the steps and looked up through the driving dust at the flag, tattered now by the flying bullets. Below was pandemonium, but now for the moment only a stray bullet sang by in its flight. Dalarge swiftly tore off the bandages from his torn hands, then suddenly leapt on to the wall and gripped the thin, double rope that led up to the flag.

As the pain bit into his bruised and wounded hands, he sobbed, but his fingers that were strong as steel claws gripped that all too thin support and pulled him upwards.

And not an Arab saw him. Within seconds he was holding on to the parapet edge, pulling himself over.

And then he was safe.

Tusin came up when the trap door was

opened. He did not look at Dalarge, crouching there. Behind him came half a dozen legionnaires, among them this time Willi Pretel and his good friend the Norwegian. And they did not look at Dalarge, either, because they had talked in his absence, yet in the end they did not know what to do.

Tusin and two legionnaires dragged the machine gun until it pointed down into the middle of the swirling mob on the parade ground; Willi Pretel and the other legionnaires crouched behind the low wall and opened fire with their Lebels.

It was slaughter, and unexpected. As the machine gun chattered, the victorious Arabs suddenly turned in rout and fled for cover. And at once their leader was able to control them again, and perhaps upbraid them for their folly in deserting their posts before victory was assured.

Once again those riflemen went back into the murk of the desert and began that deadly barrage of fire against the defenders on top of the tower. And below the Arabs took up positions in the barrack block and among the outbuildings and poured death in at the lower windows until the return fire wilted and withered and then weakened into an occasional spasmodic shot.

Corporal Tusin died, and then three legionnaires at the machine gun. And then the Norwegian slumped over his rifle, and when Willi Pretel in anguish turned him over, Odd Skadshaim just smiled for a second at his old friend and then died as so many had died that day.

Sergeant Zirko came up with more men and himself took over the machine gun. He had courage, great courage, even though his breath was bad and his heart held evil.

He fought bitterly, not understanding why it was that so suddenly the tide of Arabs had found a way through the defences. Savagely, wanting to do as much damage to his enemies as he could before dying. Because he knew that within an hour or so there would be no Sergeant Zirko on earth.

It needed but darkness, and then the Arabs would come out with flaming torches and set fire to the tower, and that would be the end to them all, even this atrocious Dalarge who had done more to destroy the fort than any man. Oh, God, that they should have been without an officer in this time of their peril. It would have been so different if Captain Paon had been there, or even Le Gros. unshapely though he was but so resolute, so capable as a leader.

But not L'Irrité. He was a mistake. He was better out of the way.

He paused while the belt was freed from a jammed cartridge, and his eyes went out to the yellow gloom of the desert. While a man lives he hopes, though reason is all against what he wishes to see.

And he saw nothing.

Someone moved at big Willi Pretel's side. It was Dalarge. 'You will speak to me, yes, Willi?' he whispered. 'You will understand, won't you? You will not avoid me as these others have done.'

Willi turned wearily and looked at the author of all their trouble. And then his face relaxed, because Willi Pretel could understand. He reached out and patted the crouching legionnaire on his shoulder, and it was like a father consoling a child who now knows that he has done terrible things and must suffer for them. For that was always Willi Pretel's way, to be a father to weaker men!

'I will speak to you, never fear, my son,' he said.

Dalarge seemed to come forward quickly, and his hand, torn open again by those rough ropes, rose trembling; it was as though there was something consoling when his fingers touched the Swiss legionnaire, as if that big man's strength flowed through and helped him.

'Always it is Willi Pretel who has the understanding,' Dalarge said, and his white face trembled into a smile and the fires seem to die for a moment from his eyes. 'If my father had been as you, Willi, think of the torment I would have been saved.' He gripped fiercely for a moment, demanding agreement with what he said. 'It isn't right that a child should be treated as I was treated. It was too much for my poor brain, was it not, Willi? Those rats — so big, so savage, and I but a weakling child. They might have killed me, but I found an old rope dangling from a beam. I used to cling to that rope with my feet drawn up beyond range of their sharp little teeth. Sometimes I seemed to hang for hours before my hard-hearted, God-fearing parents came and let me out.'

He showed his hands, and Willi tried to conceal the shudder that ran through him when he looked down on those instruments of death that had yet so far helped to save his own life.

'It gave me strength, Willi; my hands are so strong that I can climb any rope, even thin ones such as these on the flag staff. And my shoulders are strong, too, so strong. That's what it gave me, those hours in the dark cellar under the tannery — strength.'

'And it gave you the madness, my son,' said Willi softly. 'All your life you have been different, yes?'

'All my life I have been different.' There was the madness in full fire in his eyes again. 'All my life I have known that what was done to me was unjust, and all my life I have been in protest at the injustices all around me.'

'And here — there was too much?'

Dalarge crouched, his eyes narrowed against the driving dust. 'There was too much,' he whispered. 'I suffered, but I suffered more when I saw my comrades suffering under our brutal N.C.O.s. and officers. And then poor Pierre Planche he was too much for me.'

His fists clenched. 'When I saw that poor, harmless boy . . . what was left of him . . . and the way Paon rewarded the foul murderer, I vowed that he would die in the same way.' He looked at his hand and then at the flag mast with its twin ropes. 'And he did I avenged my comrade.'

'It was madness, my son . . .'

'It is madness not to protest against injustice and tyranny.' The rifle fire was rising now from the ground floor, to concentrate upon the occupants higher in the tower. That could mean one thing — the defenders down there must be nearly at an end in their earthly journey.

'And then you came and killed Le Gros

because you could not bear to hear the torture of our comrades? And then, later, you killed the brutal Sergeant Glik for the same reason?'

Dalarge nodded and kept on nodding, and he seemed to be pleased with some thought. 'It was so, my good friend. And did I not show extraordinary cunning in using an Arab weapon — a souvenir that I stole from the Englishman — when that rumour came round that the assassin was an Arab? And in leaving that window wide open so that you would not guess how I had entered the commander's room? For I wanted to live so that I could go on punishing the unjust.'

They were nearly at an end now. Two more men had died. No more than a dozen were left alive in the tower, and some of those were wounded.

Dalarge was saying, 'That Englishman, I think he knew who had killed Paon, at any rate Le Gros. It was the way he used to look at me. But he is a queer one; he does not interfere in matters which are of no concern to him — and there is little that seems to concern him.'

But Willi Pretel was looking into the yellow dust storm and wondering how many more Arabs there were out there. Now they seemed to be coming in solid line out of the fog.

He sighted his rifle.

'You are unfortunate, my son,' he said. 'You are mad, but why should that be remarkable in a world that is entirely given to madness. See, I am going to kill an Arab, a man I have never seen, a man probably who has children and a wife to depend on him, while I have none. I am going to kill him because I have been taught that way, and that way my instinct now lies. Yet is it not all madness?'

And he pulled trigger and killed a blue-coated legionnaire who was advancing on the gate.

Zirko understood it first. He was on his feet in an instant. 'It is here,' he was roaring. 'They come, our comrades from Alfia. Vive la France! We are saved!'

And yet he could not understand why it should be, how it was that news had got quickly to the coast so that, within hours, men, apparently, had marched a hundred miles across the desert to their rescue . . .

They came, brave men and disciplined, and they caught that triumphant Arab force inside the fortress and massacred them to a man, then closed the gate and manned the ramparts . . .

Zirko started to go down to welcome the new arrivals. In the trap he looked at Dalarge and said, 'My brave son, it would be better if you pitched yourself head first over the parapet. After your gallant conduct today I would not like to see you die, as die you must when I say what I saw.'

And only Dalarge heard him, because his voice was almost tender in its softness. So that only Zirko heard the reply as the legionnaire crouched like a great frog close by him.

And Dalarge said, 'It would, then, be better for you to pitch yourself down, too *mon sergent*, for I would not like to see you die, as die you must if I say what Sergeant Phare and I in my innocence saw.' He added softly, 'I do not want to die, sergeant.'

Zirko considered on the steps, and then he said, 'And I, too, do not want to die, my friend. Perhaps we will forget it, what each of us saw, yes? I do not think that your few legionnaire friends will want to remember it, either.'

When he had gone, Willi said, 'We will take you to hospital and make you well again . . . '

★　★　★

Two Arabs were there with the relief column, both mounted. One threw back the cover from his face and there was the English legionnaire named Warr. The other was a stranger.

And Warr said to Zirko that they had been but an hour on the way after stealing an Arab horse when he came upon the advancing force. Two days before they had received warning in Alfia of the impending attack, and in two days and nights the column had marched across a hundred miles of desert.

And then it was that the mystery of the gate was explained. For France has her eyes everywhere, even in the meanest village. Eyes that see and tongues that will talk if the promise of reward is sufficient

. . . men who come stealthily at appointed times to report, traitors against their own kind, but useful to an occupying power, and brave in addition.

Men with resource who take it on themselves to get through a warning message, if they see it will pay them to do so.

Such was the Arab at the gate, the Arab now calmly watching the slaughter of his own kind.

A renegade . . .

★　★　★

Sergeant Zirko solved the mystery. He came, his face black with fury, to the officer who commanded the relieving column.

His salute was a gesture of savagery. His demand was for twenty men, so that he could go into the desert immediately.

For, he explained, the fortress had fallen because of the treachery of some of the defenders. The mystery had been explained to him when he found the body of Le Groneau, shot down in the act of escaping. For over the uniform of Le

Groneau was an Arab dress.

He swore never to rest until he had brought back those traitors who had deserted at the height of battle and were now fleeing in disguise across the desert.

The officer looked out at the storm still raging and said, 'Rest, *mon sergent*. Just now it is useless. But be sure you will have your wish. You will do as you say — you will go out and bring back those wretches so that justice can be apportioned them.'

It had a familiar sound to the sergeant, that talk of justice. Ha, yes, that was how Dalarge had spoken to the Legionnaire Pretel. The good, brave, so-gallant Dalarge.

He would take him with him. And Dalarge would die by accident somehow in the desert, and then he, Sergeant Zirko, would be safe.

But perhaps that was not as the fates had ordained for the man who could climb ropes as Dalarge could . . .

THE END

We do hope that you have enjoyed reading this large print book.

Did you know that all of our titles are available for purchase?

We publish a wide range of high quality large print books including:
Romances, Mysteries, Classics
General Fiction
Non Fiction and Westerns

Special interest titles available in large print are:
The Little Oxford Dictionary
Music Book, Song Book
Hymn Book, Service Book

Also available from us courtesy of Oxford University Press:
Young Readers' Dictionary
(large print edition)
Young Readers' Thesaurus
(large print edition)

For further information or a free brochure, please contact us at:
Ulverscroft Large Print Books Ltd.,
The Green, Bradgate Road, Anstey,
Leicester, LE7 7FU, England.
Tel: (00 44) **0116 236 4325**
Fax: (00 44) **0116 234 0205**

THE LAS VEGAS AFFAIR

Norman Lazenby

Johnny Lebaron arrives in Las Vegas, leaving behind an unhappy marriage in New York. His hopes of a quiet vacation are dashed when he meets the beautiful Dulie Grande. Only recently out of jail, she seeks vengeance on the man who put her there — crooked casino owner Nat Franz. Johnny and Dulie, caught up in her vendetta against Franz, must fight for their lives against organised crime and a psychotic hit man with orders to kill them . . .

FERAL

Steve Hayes & David Whitehead

There's something not quite right about Shelby's Oasis, the tourist trap in the middle of the Arizona desert. The Shelby sisters, Agnes and Diana, have more skeletons than closets in which to hide them. And with rumours of a fortune in gold buried on the property, who can be trusted — the sisters' scheming brother Scott? The seductive Kelly-Anne? Or Mitch, the loner who stumbles into their lives? One thing's for sure: nothing at Shelby's Oasis is what it seems . . .

THE RED INSECTS

John Russell Fearn

Nick Hansley, his wife Ena and father-in-law find that their country house, 'The Cedars', radiates a positively evil aura. Their strange neighbour Dr. Lexton calls, wanting to buy their home. But who is Dr. Lexton? And as for Ena's deceased uncle, entomologist Cyrus Odder, what was the nature of the secret experiment he had worked on there? Then after a mysterious death in the house — death spreads its net across the countryside — and the entire world . . .

DEAD END

Steve Hayes & David Whitehead

Dead End, Arizona, was just another whistle-stop on the way to nowhere. But in Dead End the future of humanity depended upon the actions of a few brave souls . . . and an army of supernatural creatures with no souls at all! Earth could be invaded by another planet if they lost the war — but if they won, the battle between the living and the undead would continue . . . Either way, the streets of Dead End were going to run with blood.

FIFTY DAYS TO DOOM

E. C. Tubb

The galaxy is at war between the oxygen-breathing Terran Federation of worlds and the Ginzoes, chlorine-breathing aliens. An Earth ship is captured in battle by the Ginzoes, and its crew learns that the aliens have a newly developed catalyst. This can liberate chlorine from the sea — which, for the Ginzoes, would convert Terran worlds into suitable environments. The catalyst will be used unless the Terran Federation declares peace within fifty days. Fifty days to save Mankind . . . or fifty days to doom!